This book is an evocative gathering of short pieces from twenty-five female writers . . . This is a collection that will be appreciated by the Francophiles among us.
—*Toronto Globe and Mail*

For *Tango, an Argentine Love Story*
Tango is a remarkable addition to contemporary dharma literature. It reads like a thriller, a romance, and above all it shows the redemptive potential of a sincere spiritual practice.
—Sylvia Boorstein, PhD, author of *Happiness is an Inside Job*

The transformative power of the tango embrace beautifully captured. Bravo!
—Marina Palmer, author of *Kiss & Tango*

. . . the women in this book offer a useful perspective, highly flavored, with engaging erotic implications . . . great voyeuristic fun.
—Herbert Gold, author of *Haiti: Best Nightmare on Earth, Bohemia, Fathers,* and *A Girl of Forty*

Praise for Camille Cusumano's books

For *The Mystique of the Last Cannoli*
"A delightfully engaging romp that weaves together the bonds of Sicilian sisterhood and family secrets across two continents. *Perfetto per la spiaggia!*"
—Carla Gambescia, author of *La Dolce Vita University: An Unconventional Guide to Italian Culture from A to Z*

For *The Last Cannoli*
Attests to the power of storytelling to hold life together through all its diasporas.
—Lawrence Ferlinghetti, San Francisco Poet Laureate

Cannoli . . . is a lyrical, exuberant novel about an Italian American family facing an increasingly homogenized society.
—Laura A. Salsin, *Italian Americana*

For *Wilderness Begins at Home (Travels with my big Sicilian family)*
Whether they're fighting off a wild bear or dealing with a clandestine coffee fetish, sitting Zen or locking horns with a Voodoo Priestess, Camille and her lively family share fun and mischief around the world.
—Laurie McAndish King, author of *Lost, Kidnapped, Eaten Alive! True stories from a curious traveler.*

For *Italy, A Love Story*
Cusumano has put together an outstanding volume of women's travel writing, demonstrating a fullness of living. This collection is a page-turner.
—Carol Bonomo Albright, editor of *Italian Americana*

Camille Cusumano has assembled a unique cast of
women writing about their encounters with Italy.
Together, they come close to defining that indefinable
something—the people, the culture, the fit of people and
culture with their landscape—that draws the traveler
again and again to this land.
—Lawrence DiStasi, Editor of *Una Storia Segreta, When
    Italian Americans Were Enemy Aliens*

A multi-faceted look at the charms of the popular
Mediterranean country through the eyes of twenty-eight
noted women writers. They contribute appealing personal
stories of their travels to various parts of the country.
—*Santa Barbara News-Press*

For *France, A Love Story*
This is a very readable collection . . . Tales are alternately
loving, witty, nostalgic, and yes, occasionally swooning.
—*San Francisco Chronicle*

In this beautiful collection, women share their experiences
firsthand, reflecting on the ways France's unique culture
has enriched and enchanted their lives.
—*France Today*

The heart of this book is in the maturity of its voices of
experience.
—*Boston Globe*

The Mystique of
the Last Cannoli

The Mystique of the Last Cannoli

CAMILLE CUSUMANO

Centanni Publications
San Francisco, California

The Mystique of the Last Cannoli

Cover photo: Kathleen Hennessy McGee
Published by: Centanni Publications
Information, comments, praise, criticism, or requests for per-
mission to reprint: ocaramia2000@gmail.com

CATALOGING IN PUBLICATION DATA:
The Mystique of the Last Cannoli by Camille Cusmano

ISBN: 979-8-994157817

First Printing 2026

For my Father,
Charles Anthony Cusumano
who, after his ten biological kids flew the nest,
sought to adopt six girls
and four boys

Donitella Family Tree

Gemma Leonforte & Franco Coniglio m. 1920

Lucia Conforti & Mario Donitella m. 1915

Madgalena Coniglio & Vincent Donitella m. 1941

Mario b. 1942

Lucy b. 1944

Vinnie b.1946

Carmine b. 1948

Frankie b. 1949

Madeleine b. 1954, d. 1970

Rena b. 1955

Maria b. 1958

Teresa b. 1959

Carmela b. 1963

Prologue

Carmela Donitella's parents' home, Rahway, New Jersey
Thursday, October 31, 1985, Halloween

*Carmela opens a big refrigerator's freezer. She pulls out
a cannoli, the one she believes goes back to 1941. The
cannoli in her open palm is wrapped in white veil and
plastic, with a layer of frost on it sparkling like tiny
diamonds. She is crystal gazing.*

We have a family ritual of saving the Last Cannoli,
since 1941, the year Mom and Dad married. It's been
kept frozen. It has become sacred with time, as rituals are
apt to do. Miraculously the confection never deteriorates.
It brings luck, usually. Except that year Madeleine died.
Even when other foods in the freezer go south the Last
Cannoli survives, magically keeping its integrity. What is
frozen is time, my family story. Within that gelid sweet, a
story from long before I was born. This is the mystery of
the Last Cannoli.
   This year I, the youngest of ten, will seek to defrost time
and words. Inspired by my father's desire for ten more
children, I will solve the mystique and mystery of
the Last Cannoli.

She carefully replaces the cannoli in the freezer.

Please, dear Madeleine, help us help Dad get the Mariners
Mansion, a buck, and thousands more.

Friday, November 1, 1985, All Saints' Day

It was the time of year when everything went dry and brittle, the grass, the trees, the leaves, air. Even skin and hair and eyes seemed ready to shed their outer layers. And the world seemed to be ready and waiting for its papery husk to fall away, so it could lie down in a pile of raked leaves and sleep, sleep, sleep.

This afternoon my father drove down to Broadview, past his old dinky produce stand. Then for old time's sake through Elmora, a part of Elizabeth where some of his Sicilian aunts and uncles lived. Finally we drove to the Port to see the old Mariners Mansion near where his father's spirit once appeared to him. Dad wanted to visit the ruins of the once solid old building he dreamed of buying for a buck and renovating for the cost of his soul.

The mansion, though run-down and vandalized, was big with high ceilings and old chandeliers. Broken windows like dimmed eyes or empty sockets my father wanted to breathe life into. The foundation was strong.

Now the wrecker's ball would probably level it. A shame. We had come to see it one last time, like other last times, like saying good-bye to a dream that never got realized. But still hoping. He'd dreamed dreams before, ten times at least, one after each child was born.

In one version of his dream, Dad would open a little restaurant on the bottom level of the Mariners Mansion. He and my brothers liked to cook, more so than Mom and my sisters. "The gastronomical gene is obviously on the father's side," Mom said cavalierly. The kitchen was big enough to cook for many more than ten boys and girls. The dark and empty shell was now a hangout for juvenile delinquents. Broken glass, graffiti, sexual paraphernalia desecrated its venerable history. My father threw a rock through one of the broken windows.

A shell, crumbling, I thought. We moved on.

"Right there," he said, pointing to a weedy field. "I used to go in that field with my mother and get *cicoria*." My parents grew up when Elizabeth, Peterstown enclave in particular, had more weedy fields.

"Cheekoria?"

"Yeah, *cicoria*, you know, the chicory. The *scarol'*."

"Oh, yeah, scod-all, the one we like with meatballs and kidney beans."

"That's it, *scarol'*. Sometimes on the way back from a party with the Bellinos and Noceras, we picked *cardun'* on the railroad tracks on Morris Avenue."

"*God-dunes*?"

"Yes. My mother used to send for the fresh ones from the lady over on Fourth and Amity. No, it was Second. Dimayo was her name. She was light in the head. Old Carmela, your namesake, sells them too." She was sharp as a tack forged yesterday. Old Carmela had psychic powers.

Since I'd been helping my father with his business, I knew that *god-dunes* were really *cardoni* to Italians, cardoons to Americans, who were just discovering the wild delicacy, although they didn't know where or how to harvest it.

My father hurled more small rocks and a few Sicilian curses at the old broken-down would-be orphanage. Some hoodlums cursed as they were roused out of their illicit activity, whatever that may have been. He returned the curse in his dialect, acting as if he were a cop. "Come out with your hands up." Only I knew his joking voice. He did have a nightstick in the car. "Or I'll smoke yuz out."

The mansion symbolized all the kids he never had and all the dreams he had forsaken for the ten he did have. He wanted more after I, tenth and last, was born. My mother put her foot down for the first time in her life. But not the last. He had wanted to visit Old Carmela, my godmother who was a tea-leaf reader, to see if Mom could get pregnant again.

Mom said Dad hadn't fulfilled his dreams because "we were busy manufacturing you kids." Mom's dreams, of being married to Dad and having ten healthy babies, always seemed to have been satisfied in her life.

Dad used to say his latest dream out loud like a drill he had to memorize. He went through the entire renovation of the building from the ground floor up. The chandeliers, the kitchen big enough for him, my mother, and my brothers—the best cooks—to prepare food for all the orphans he planned to bring there. The sleeping arrangements. The curriculum for teaching the kids, everything from reading and writing to cooking, dancing, and speaking Sicilian.

"Maybe we should draft the local juvenile delinquents for our first group of inmates, Dad," I said loud enough to be heard by them.

"Ah, we have another place for delinquents," Dad yelled back to me.

I used to listen to Dad's dream and go through the roll call in my head with him so that I knew right where I'd put my own feet and my head. I felt like hurling a few rocks myself. The wrecker's ball be damned.

It was All Saints', a holy day of obligation, so we headed to St. Anthony's to catch the afternoon mass. I would sit in a pew and gather wool or daydream while Dad prayed to all the saints. But especially to St. Jude, protector of children.

Following the mass this melancholic autumn day, my father took me to the dentist in Peterstown. Afterward we drove a little bit out of our way. I wasn't sure why.

"Your tooth still hurt, Cat?" he asked.

"It's a lot better," I said.

"How about a little shot of whiskey, Cat, to make it all better?"

"Dad, I'm not teething." My oldest sister Lucy rubbed whiskey on the kids' gums when they teethed. She carried on the family legacy, not just soothing gums the way our grandparents taught us, but "manufacturing" kids.

"You stayed home from school, so it must've been bad."

"I don't student-teach on Fridays—and besides, Catholic

schools are closed today."

"When you start for real?"

"Mother Seton needs an English teacher in January."

"Hey, that's something to celebrate . . . a girls' Catholic high."

It was. Teaching at an all-girls Catholic high would be a change from Blessed Sacrament grammar school. I noticed my father was driving toward the Villa Roma. So I said, "I don't mind if you want to stop and say hello to Big Frank."

"That-a girl, Cat," he said. When he called me Cat that meant he was in a pretty good mood. He said I slinked into a room full of people unseen. I liked when he was a good mood. He whistled "Oh, Marie" and turned our big Chrysler station wagon with its ostentatious tailfins down Stiles Street toward the Villa Roma. On radio WNEW, William B. Williams was playing a Patti Page song. I wished we had FM radio in the car to play my music—gone were the days of rock on AM radio. Dad still didn't think rock would last, even after all its years of evolving. Even though his oldest son, my brother Mario, had had a successful run in the rock band SilkTones before turning full time to science.

At the Villa Roma, I asked for anisette instead of whiskey and went to sit at a table to read the Newark *Star-Ledger* that was lying there. I knew my father would get talking with Big Frank, as we called my brother Frankie's godfather. They'd forget I was there. The news was boring and I was half listening to Frank and Dad. Even though they switched to Sicilian once in a while, I got their drift.

Dad was having financial problems and would never talk

to anyone else outside the family about it. Frank was like family because he stood up for Frankie at his baptism. I'd only been learning vaguely about the problem over the months, catching snippets of conversation, reading looks between my parents.

My father's produce business had been audited and he was told he had to pay back taxes on the new bigger structure. I didn't know how much, but enough to make my parents stay up late and talk. The mistake in reporting seemed to surface after Ralph Giordano, Dad's friend who owned the land, let Dad lease it for a song. It was a case of the venerable Italian practice of one hand washes the other. Dad had helped keep Ralph's teenage son and his friend out of juvenile detention. The boys had gone on a robbing spree, mostly nonviolent pickpocketing. Dad went to court as a character witness and agreed to sponsor the boys doing community service and working after school at his old stand. He paid them a wage and they seemed to be walking the straight and narrow since. Dad was like a poor man's Godfather.

Back taxes were not his real problem, or so I gathered. But I was not sure what was. Recently, Ralph had gone to jail. I didn't know why but it upset my parents. I only knew of it because a cousin two years older had told me.

My mother prayed the rosary more than usual. She bit the back of her hand like she did in the old days, or so I'm told. The last time she prayed and bit the back of her hand this often was when Khrushchev said he was going to drop a bomb on America. I was not alive for this. I only knew about it, like so many other things, because my nine (now eight) older siblings had told me.

My father sat on a stool at the bar in the darkness. I felt cradled and safe in my own world. I saw old pictures tacked up on the wall above me. In the rogues' gallery of glossy color photos of Barbie and Ken–style brides and grooms were Pope John XXIII and Pope John Paul II.

A guy walked in and Frank turned over his shoulder from the register and stared, then said an unfriendly "Howdy."

I knew it was Sammy Bono from the Berg or Peterstown, the Italian enclave. My parents talked about him—they would forget I was there. Just as they did about Uncle Ralph, also a goombah. Ralph used to pay Mom and Dad to let him use our telephone on Sundays. He would take the receiver into the bathroom and close the door. Usually he was in there an hour. Later Rena told me he was running numbers. I didn't know exactly what that meant at the time, only that it was illegal but not necessarily bad. I gathered that my parents didn't think Ralph was bad for going to jail. He just got caught doing something illegal. Maybe I was surmising too much.

I had heard my father say to my mother just the other day, "I never liked his kind." They were talking about Sammy. I knew Sam, unlike Ralph, was just a bad egg and it had something to do with Ralph.

"Have you thought about my request, Vinnie," Sammy Bono now asked my father. Dad made a sound of disgust, one I imagine he learned to make long ago as a kid.

"You know who you're talking to?" my father asked. It was not exactly the authoritative voice he used with his kids. Frank had already lined up another drink without being asked.

I couldn't hear their entire conversation from where I sat at this table, feigning interest in the news. But I already knew, from hearing Frank and Dad the last time I was here, that Sammy wanted my father to store some goods he came into—one of those they-fell-off-a-truck stories—somewhere at Dad's newly remodeled produce stand.

Every now and then their voices got loud enough for me to hear clearly.

"C'mon fellas, what are you intimating? Hey, I tried to catch the driver," Bono was saying. "I couldn't even get his license plate. You know the traffic on Bayway Circle. Crazy, gotta talk to the mayor about that. Vinnie?"

"Some problems even the mayor can't fix," Frank said.

"I even stopped at St. Anthony's," Sammy said, "to pray for guidance from up above." That registered like sacrilege. My parents were married in St. Anthony's.

My father was silent. And I knew and Frank knew that was never good. It was always better when my father was talking. So much for his good mood.

"So, what do you want with my guidance then, Boner?"

My father spoke through his teeth. "I'm not exactly Divine Providence."

"I know," said Bono. "You're better." His voice went low. "You got all that warehouse space."

"Divine Prov got heaven and then some," my father said.

"Not like your new place, which is more ideal than heaven on earth."

Frank was getting nervous. He was drying glasses he had already dried.

"Frank," Sam said sarcastically, "I think those glasses are dry now."

"My space ain't for rent," said my father.

"I'm not talking about renting," said Bono. "Anyway, I'm feeling generous, give you 48 hours to think about it."

"You should've asked me 48 years ago before I was married, when I was young and naïve and ready to believe in the fast fix. You ham'n'egger. Go pound salt."

That last was Dad's final salute to anyone from a bad driver to a strong-arming hood.

Bono frowned, said nothing, just took off his wristwatch, a shiny gold one, and put it in my father's hand. "Here's 2,000 clams' worth of precious hardware, 17 jewels, Swiss precision. While you think about it."

Bono turned and made for the door. My father let the watch dangle from his hand, his elbows leaning back on the bar. Then just as the front door was closing, Dad yelled, "Boner!" and Bono turned and Frank was saying, "Quick! Think fast!" Sam wasn't thinking fast enough as the gold watch flew through the air and met the side of his head, knocking his hat askew.

"You forgot something," my father said as Sam picked up the watch, never taking his eyes off Dad.

"This time I asked." Sam threw the watch on the bar and straightened his fedora. Did I mention that, like the good-for-nothing two-bit hood he was, he never took his hat off. Frank picked up the watch as if it were the culprit. He shoved it under the bar.

"Scum," my father said a few minutes after Sam was gone. He laughed when he said it, a genuine little laugh not colored with any fear. The money really was the least of his problems.

"He's got nerve," Frank said.

"He's got me by the balls is what he's got," my father said. "He's my new landlord, and he's got me over a barrel."

I was flabbergasted. As far as I knew, it was goombah Ralph who owned the land and had let my father set up on it essentially for free.

In the car heading home, I said, "Dad, let's stop by Bella Palermo—I'd like to pick up a cannoli."

"Why, Cat, some special occasion?" We usually had cannoli only once a year, at Thanksgiving.

"No, it's just that I dreamed about one . . . that is, Madeleine appeared in my dream and all I can recall is her saying something about the Last Cannoli. So, in memory of her."

"Maybe she was trying to tell you everything is going to be hunky dory."

"Maybe."

I wondered if he believed that.

Saturday, November 2

Like the Cat my father said I was I slipped unseen, unheard in the front door, never locked, of our Donitella home. The percolating coffee made more sound than I did. Ah, that familiar aroma. It was early so my parents were in their bedroom getting dressed, the door ajar. What I heard was a scene from Shakespeare if he had been *Siciliano*:

VINCENT
Sono sicuro che gli orologi siano stati nascosti, forse durante la notte. Non riesco a capire dove sono nascosti.

(I'm sure the watches have been stashed, maybe during the night. I can't figure out where they're hidden.)

MAGDALENA
Di semplicemente al prosciutto e all'uovo di pestare il sale.
(Just tell the ham 'n' egger to go pound salt.)

VINCENT
(In a weepy voice)
Ho gia. Come faro ad avere la villa con un crimine che incombe sulla mia testa? . .

(I already have. How am I gonna get the mansion with a crime hanging over my head.)

"Don't tell me," my mother said. "He wants to adopt ten more."

I found my mother in the backyard of our childhood home on Creek Street in Rahway, where 12 of us once fit snugly. She was tending to her winter garden of Swiss chard, broccoli rabe, dandelions, and bulb fennel. Drying vines on the ground attested to the beefsteak tomatoes, long gone and preserved in mason jars. I had thought I was bringing my mother news.

"You knew about this?"

"Last month it was the priesthood. This month ten more kids."

"What? Dad a priest? Taking vows of chastity, obedience, silence? *My* dad?"

My mother pulled up a whole fennel plant. "You didn't hear us arguing? He wanted to join a silent branch of monks. Can you imagine your father keeping quiet for a day, no less a week, a month." She shook the fennel vigorously to remove¬ soil from the roots.

"Guess he's moving away from his worldly ways."

My mother made a sound like *Don't kid yourself.* "He's been reading *The Seven Storey Mountain* by Thomas Merton about his conversion to Catholicism. Now he wants to join that monastery, Gethsemani, in Kentucky."

"Don't they make bourbon there?"

"As a matter of fact. Now he wants me to be like I was at 19, blissfully ignorant, starting from scratch—with ten adoptees."

"You know about the would-be orphanage then—down the Port? For a buck plus what, how many tens of thousands to renovate?"

"He was away the first two years I had your brother." My mother was still thinking of the early days of their marriage in 1941 when Dad was sent to the South Pacific after Pearl Harbor. "He wants us to change roles. He wants to do the mothering, the nurturing. I'm to be the disciplinarian."

"That's hilarious, Mom. I can see Dad getting soft. But I can't see you getting tough." Although I had to admit, but didn't say, she had come back changed from her solo trip to Sicily a few years ago. Still clearly in love with Dad, the man who once held her down, to paraphrase the Stones. But feistier, quicker to speak her mind. No longer just the submissive housewife she had been during our upbringing.

She sighed and said, "He thinks he was too hard, I was too soft."

"Might be true—but it's all water under the bridge as they say. We're all flowing along swimmingly. Don't you think?"

"And too, your father notices how I've changed since that Sicilian vacation."

"What was it about Sicily that changed you? Was it the ricotta? Those creamy curds?"

Mom laughed. She had told us more than once that the Polly-O brand of ricotta we used and loved was many notches below the ricotta she tasted one day in the country-side of that Mediterranean island. It seemed to have opened more than her taste buds to new vistas. "The soil, the grass, the air, the cow, its moo—the whole pipeline is just different there."

"You are . . . more . . . liberal-minded, open, expressing your own opinions, not Dad's. I'd've thought you'd have come back more, shall I say traditional?"

"Me too . . . I don't know exactly." She stopped weeding, took off her gloves. "This I know: having to attend to you ten kids all the time—don't misunderstand—I loved being a mother. I love your father. But. The *but*." She sat back on her heels. "I never realized until I was alone in the land of my parents. For the first time in my life, I was so fully present, whether walking the farmland, hulling beans with my cousin, eating the pasta al forno, the rabbit with wild mushrooms, the free-range fowl, wonderful repasts . . ."

Mom seemed to be doing a soliloquy about what is truly precious. Time. Life. "I know those are commonplace thoughts, but there was a single moment . . ."

She went on a long time and I could almost see the verdant hills and craggy outcroppings of Sicily where I had yet to set foot. And my mother shedding her outer skin—like the beans she was hulling with her cousin—finding out who she was. She stopped and put her gloves back on and started to weed again.

I studied my mother, who at 63 had stopped dyeing her hair and kept it smartly coiffed. Her skin was still smooth and her back erect. After a moment, when she seemed to return to New Jersey, I had to ask. "So who are you?"

She didn't skip a beat. "I'm your mother! What a question."

I wondered if she even knew I was there as she rhapsodized about her moment, her epiphany, in Sicily, where she'd gone alone after Madeleine died.

"What do you plan to do with the finocchio?" I asked.

"Your father wants to try some new recipe to share with your brother Frankie for his restaurant."

"Dad's a pretty good cook, Mom, you have to admit."

"I'll give him that. He passed that gift on to his sons. He was more inventive than I was. Sometimes too creative. I was mostly concerned with getting enough good food prepared for the 12 of us."

Mom was glad that Dad had the luxury of being innovative. She said he was planning a typical Sicilian feast, a pasta pomodoro with eggplant Parm and braised fennel for a visiting nun who would stay with them a few days. He wanted to impress Sister Julieta because she was a friend of his cousin's daughter, also a nun, in Sicily.

"A feast in return for her prayers for his soul?" I asked.

"He likes to get all the help he can get. Sister Julieta and Sister Assumption met doing work in an orphanage in Nairobi."

"That should be interesting for Dad. Julieta can give him advice on orphans."

"That could be worrisome."

"Oh?"

"If he comes to me next with a desire to go volunteer in Nairobi."

"Perish the thought."

I wanted to probe more into my father's past, what accounted for his dark streak. During our growing-up years—at least mine, as I could attest—my father was often fun, funny, poetic, a great storyteller, and mostly charismatic.

When we packed the old Chrysler station wagon on Sundays and traveled, my father frequently broke into songs, some of which he had made up decades ago (including "We Are the Donitellas" sung with a bit of irony to the Irish tune of "McNamara's Band"). In his younger days, according to my older siblings, his moods could turn on a dime. His dark ones were hellish, but when they were good, all was right with the world. Then he would express his love for us kids and our mother, often with hyperbole—he "loved us more than life itself." He told the little kids funny stories ("The world will end when there are no more Popsicle sticks") and led us through sing-alongs ("Oh, Marie" and "Bill Grogan's Goat" were some of his favorites). He wrote love songs to my mother after he had tested her good nature by making difficult demands, usually some sort of gag order—*Don't question my authority, you are my wife, destined to love, honor, and obey me.* Even as a kid, I could recall once when his charismatic side was fully engaged. As my mother perused the souvenirs in a shop down the shore, he and the store owner, an Italian named Giolini, entertained patrons with an old Italian folk song, "Quel Mazzolin di fiori." At another shop, he admonished a guard, "Stop whistling and sing through your mouth!" Together they broke into "When the Saints Go Marching In."

But then he had a brooding side, dark moods. He was punitive, unbudging about his rules of the family. Being on time for supper, attending family affairs together, not questioning his authority, being polite. He used to yell at the TV's female announcers to "go home and have babies." He made no bones about his belief that with women in the workplace the world was in a downward spiral. But now that he had seen four of his six daughters develop into accomplished professionals (me too, someday soon), he had softened. Not by any stretch of the imagination a feminist. But it was a quantum leap of progress for him to allow his daughters to be Ms., not Miss or Mrs.

"What to do about Dad and his desire for ten more younglings?"

"Not a thing. He'll either fulfill his latest dream or add it to the stockpile of the rest of the unfulfilled dreams. And, most likely, go on dreaming. Next to raising kids, he is best at that."

Magdalena in Sicily

Late spring, some years after my daughter went to sleep and woke up on the other side, I packed my bags and headed to the other side of the ocean . . . [her voice cracks] I learned that the pain of loss, if you have a body to lay in the ground, changes into something bearable. A jewel box of memories, a safe of valuables that need never be cashed in, a mental chapel of quiet and solitude in which to pray.

I found for the first time in my life that a remedy rests in thinking of oneself. I stopped in Paris to fulfill a dream in a half ounce of fragrance. Then in a church I lit the extra-large votive candle and raised my eyes to the statue of the Magdalen being lifted to heaven by two angels. I gave Madeleine her name, our name, and she never even got to know forbidden pleasures. She may have been an average beauty, but her soul was as radiant as a smile, as candlelight. Pure as the sound of running water in the nearby fountain of that Place de la Concorde. I blessed myself with holy water and left the dimly lit church.

One of the little miracles of life was that I had stumbled upon the Church of the Madeleine on my way to buy my fragrance. I continued down the rue Faubourg Saint-Honoré and found the parfumerie. Even before the storekeeper explained that Chanel No. 5 was Coco's fifth attempt—as Madeleine was my sixth—I knew what I would do.

I took that small, gorgeously carved bottle to the new bridge, the one with the gargoyles. I stood dead center and stared down at the opaque, swift-moving water. I dabbed five pulses—wrists, temples, heart—and poured Coco's fifth child into the Seine, in honor of my sixth. I offered a prayer of thanks to both Marys who had given me what a mother wants to feel about her lost child: that I had nothing else to give her.

I stashed the empty bottle.

I was in Paris because my daughter taught me what I should have taught her, that dreams are as God-given as the prayers we grace his house with. "Mom, I'm always running through the house, up and down, up and down, all three floors," Madeleine had told me. "I'm finding passages and rooms that were never there before, that we never knew about. Sometimes it's fun, like I'm on the verge of finding a treasure chest, and sometimes . . . I'm so scared, there's some dark figure there, coming to get me, and I want to scream and I'm not able to."

By the time I realized Madeleine was telling me about a dream, my husband was calling my name as he'd had his own nightmare, and I forgot what I wanted to tell her. Even now, I can't recall what it was I could have said to set her free. But then the doctor said there was no way . . . A bulging vessel is a ticking time bomb.

I boarded a succession of trains, finally settling in for a long ride on the all-night train from Rome to Palermo. I called it the Steam Special. It was hot and humid, and the passengers were jam-packed like loaves of fast-rising dough. The wheels clacked and clicked like an old skeleton. I felt so many eyes on me, a middle-aged woman without a man, dressed in colors, pantsuits, and skirts with scarves, hair cropped and dyed auburn, styled, and sprayed.

The fat silver-haired man next to me whose legs seemed to swell with each rock of the car must have thought I was done up for him. His sausage hands keep "falling" on my thigh. After the third time I said, "Signor, prego!" And a few choice words only my potty-mouthed mother would have used. He retracted his hand and smiled as if his touch were an accident. I caught the gleam in the dark eyes of a tall young Italian in his army uniform, no doubt on liberty. He invited me to catch some air in the corridor.

"I heard you speak Sicilian, Signora, but you look anything but."

"Oh, I'm a hundred percent, Signor . . . ?"

"Antonio—Tony, call me."

"Magdalena, Tony. I'm just born on the other side of the

ocean. What's with that guy?"

"Who? The man sitting next to you? Nothing. He's Sicilian. And you, you are una donna sola."

"I get it. The laws of nature. How could I forget."

Between my Sicilian and Tony's broken English we got acquainted. Tony was on leave to see his wife. He would be getting off and heading to Naples before the train crossed the Messina Strait. One of the nearby cars emptied out, so we sat there away from Mr. Roman Hands. Just as I finished telling Tony I don't know why Italians think all American women are loose, he slipped his arm around my shoulders. I let it stay there. He said, "I should say good-bye. My stop is coming soon."

"Good-bye, Tony. As I told you I'm a mother of ten and a grandmother . . ." The air blast smothered my words as we entered another long tunnel through rocky mountain and his lips pressed on mine. It was the longest tunnel. And the sweetest, most uncomplicated kiss I had had in a long time.

Even the rocks, even the wind sang. What did they say?

As I twirled macaroni with my husband's first cousins they compared the faces of my children in photos I had brought to faces in an old photo. We marveled at how a smile can travel forever through time, down a bloodline. We feasted on pasta al forno, eggplant in tomato sauce with many toes of soft garlic, farm vegetables slathered thick and fragrant with green olive oil, pizza with anchovies.

Rosalia Franciamore was second cousin to my mother. "God sent us to each other," she said and cried and laughed *and hugged me so tightly. Rosalia, her brother Carlo, and I dined simply but royally our first evening alone on pasta fazool, bread, and salad greens dipped in olive oil and vinegar. Carlo was quiet and hardly looked at me, but his presence was imposing. He was at least ten years younger than me, handsome and firmly muscled from field work. Rosalia set out pastries that preserved the old memory of hardship and suffering of women on this island—the eyes of St. Lucy, the breasts of St. Agatha, and the bones of St. Rosalia. The virgin's creamy breasts were too rich for me, the sugary marzipan bones best left to ossify as platter ornaments. But St. Lucy's dry, crumbly eyes were perfect. We dunked them in espresso, and I savored not for the first time in my life the marriage of sweet and bitter. I told my cousins how Madeleine died, like her grandfather years before, on the feast of St. Lucy, December 13.*

"E brutta la morta di un' carissima, è vero." *Rosalia pronounced the horror of losing a dear one as she has known it herself. But I saw she was too emotional to speak of it yet. I calmly explained about finding my child asleep like porcelain, white as the sheets, cold as marble. I'd never spoken of this yet and somehow saying it in Sicilian was easier, as if part of me were observing she who grieved.*

Carlo drove me up Monte Cammarata. He cursed at other drivers and said at last, "Du' cosi no potti addrizzari lu Signore li cucuz' e li testi duri." *I knew this Sicilian proverb well—two things the Lord can't straighten out,* cucuzza *and hard heads. My easily irritated mother said it often.*

At the mountaintop, he parked his car and wanted to kiss like lovers. "We are too close," I said.

"Cuggina, *no, not so close enough,*" he smiled. "*You stay, Magdalena, and marry me.*"

"*Wow, a marriage proposal. I haven't had one since 1941,*" I said, "*unless you count my son Vinnie's proposal when he was ten.*"

"*I be good husband, Magdalena. I wait for woman like you all my life, who is beautiful, wise, and* cento porcento Siciliana.*"

"*Yes, 100 percent Sicilian.*" The very thought of staying, being who I was these past weeks, rolling with the seasons, was intoxicating beyond my wildest dream.

"*I have a husband, a family.*"

"*What kind of man lets you alone?*"

A sad man, a down man.

"*You know Carlo, there's a lot of uncertainty in America . . . and it gets some people down.*"

"*But not you,* bella *Magdalena. You are up and the most beautiful woman I ever see. Your husband is the luckiest man in the world.*"

And he knows it. I think. A thousand ideas and thoughts of life without my children and grandchildren raced through my head.

"*Take me down the mountain, Carlo,*" I said.

I stared at the tomato paste, the strattu *drying in the sun with flies all around it and recalled how I had asked Madeleine to go down the cellar and get me a jar of canned tomatoes. She came bounding up the stairs with the jar and said, "I'm not afraid to go down there alone anymore, Ma, I haven't had my dream in a long time." I looked at her and tried to remember her dream.*

I knew my kids thought because I was always doing, always cooking, cleaning, moving furniture, making shopping lists, worrying about their father, that I didn't notice little things. But I still remember her face. That peaceful look might have made a less observant mother happy. But I had seen that look only once before. Nonnie. After she stopped feeling the pain in her torso, right before she passed at age 92. And so I felt disturbed about what Madeleine said to me next. "Ma, I'm thinking I might want to enter the novitiate."

I knew all about God's calling of the chosen few. But still, I couldn't help but feel she was called because I had failed her somehow. How I wished now that I had asked, What kind of bargain did you make with God? What's his dowry? How I wished I had said, You don't have to give up so much yet. I was thinking of my younger self maybe. Of course, I couldn't speak this thought, or even hear it, until long after she was gone. Even now, I am still trying to make sense of God's will.

Sitting with Rosalia and the other women, I found myself thinking more broadly than usual, having two tongues at my disposal. One of the women rose to stir the crimson mass of strattu *that sat on its wooden plank near an open window. Flies swarmed the thick paste. I knew that it was the remains of tomatoes peeled, seeded, and drying in the sun, several bushels of them that had fully expressed themselves down to their essential sweetness. Like my daughter, an apple of gold. She was part of the carbon cycle now, her sister Rena, studying her biology, had told me,*

*helping me to revise my idea about heaven, having learned
something of living hell.*

*I wished I had my daughters with me . . . I was for the
first time in my life so fully present and aware of what was
precious. I sensed with equal amounts of bliss and grief that
as each moment slipped away, something was lost never to
be regained. How could I ever, ever hope to carry home to
my loved ones these moments with Carlo and Rosalia, who
had yet to speak her losses to me? Bearing children was
divine, but this, bearing myself—shedding layer after layer
of dead skin to find out who I was—was even more so.*

Amen.

Sunday, November 3

Sometime before I was born, Dad had one brief affair. She was a blond. It was long ago. It occurred between kids numbers four and five, or maybe five and six. I can't keep others' memories straight sometimes. It's one of the family secrets hiding in plain sight, one of the not-discussed wounds. Mom forgave Dad. She thinks Dad has not forgiven himself—a form of auto-punishment. The kids who knew thought she was too tired to do anything else. Eventually after number six, Madeleine, died, Mom went to Sicily and as far as my sisters knew she had one special kiss there, details under wraps—now a special memory to be shared at her pleasure.

This Sunday afternoon Mom gathered my sisters and me. Unexpectedly, she agreed to tell us how LouAnn, her new best friend, came unbidden into her life just a few months ago. As Mom spoke, I couldn't help but notice how different her voice was from when Dad and my brothers were around. She sounded like my mother with a new twist.

Magdalena and LouAnn

I saw this blond coming slowly up the walk to our front door. I was thinking conspiracy, not mere coincidence that one of the topics of the day happened to be that blond from long ago.

My husband of 44 years was telling me he wanted to be a priest. He wanted me to give him leave of our marriage vows, just temporary, so he could join some order of no talkies. Your father, who talks a streak when awake, twists and shouts in his sleep on a rolling basis.

"The brothers will have to muzzle you at night," I tried. He looked so beaten when he got this brainy idea of his. He thought he didn't deserve the pleasure of the flesh anymore. He was still taking it on the chin over and over about that blond years ago. I had told him, "Me and God, we're over it, getting on with our lives. You gotta forgive yourself." But no, my husband wanted a hair shirt, saltpeter, and whatever immolation of the flesh was "in" these days.

So what was that blond doing looking at my front door. I was fit to be tied. Don't tell me. Her, too, coming to beg my forgiveness. Madonna mia. They were both gonna kill me with their own contrition. I always said, cheating was its own punishment.

Du' cosi no potti addrizzari lu Signore li cucuz' e li testi duri, two things the Lord can't straighten out—cucuzza and hard heads.

"It would just be for a year," he said, "every day I would pray for my family . . . The kids are on their own . . . the grandkids . . . you don't seem to need me anymore like you

used . . . You made that trip to Sicily all alone."

"Stop that. That trip is over. Maybe that's what you need—why don't we go again?" I was losing my patience and concentration with the blond outside our house looking in like she was selling something, God knew what. Maybe she was a stray Witness. They mostly detour away from this house, probably thinking the body of a Jehovah who went AWOL was actually buried in our cellar, a tale worthy of your father.

Whatever Goldilocks was up to, I was thinking adversary, not ally. At last she got up the courage to ring the doorbell.

"Yes?" I hissed, frosty.

"Hello, I'm sorry to bother you. Is this the Donitella residence?"

"Yes, it is." Frostier yet.

"Look, I'm sorry if it's a bad time . . . does Vincent Donitella . . . I'm LouAnn Harris. I was married to Buddy Higgins. He was killed in 1943 in New Guinea, where Vincent—he might be your husband?"

"Oh, of course. Come in. I've heard my husband mention Buddy's name."

There in that little parlor where you kids and your friends slept on summer nights, where years ago Nonnie rocked her soul into the next world, your father got his war demons handed to him.

"Have a seat," I told her kindly.

"Where to start." LouAnn smiled and suddenly she didn't look so hard and brassy to me. I could see she had been a beauty and still was quite attractive with her skin lined in the right places, like someone worn from work, not petty

worry, her hair cropped and out of the way like my own.

Your father said, "I knew Buddy . . ."

"You were his best friend," LouAnn started in. "I was not the whore they said. But I'll get to that." I liked this girl, how she came in like a lamb and then got her lioness voice good and strong. God knows I needed her that day.

She presented a box to Vincent in which were two items, a bound manuscript in an old blue folder and a medallion, which upon inspection turned out to be a Medal of Honor.

"Sir, you are the one who deserves that, not Buddy Higgins. I'm sorry it's so late in coming, but all these years I never wanted to read, had no interest in his war diary. Now I know why. I had no idea it was yours. I only opened it for the first time a few days ago."

"I never wanted to see it again," said Vincent, paging through without reading it.

He let me take it from him and flip through. The pages were as yellow as nicotined fingers. I recognized that crooked typeface instantly.

"Why didn't you keep this?" I asked him. "It's a precious document." To which he gave me that look where he no longer had to say its tired refrain, You ask too many questions. I opened it and started to read. But I quickly closed it.

I knew I had the good luck to meet LouAnn in the flesh before I met her in this booklet as a falsely accused philandering wife more than 40 years ago.

"I don't want this medal, miss."

"You should take it. We both know what our country gives this medal for—gallantry, the risk of life above and

beyond the call of duty in an armed conflict in which the United States is not a belligerent party. I repeat, in which the United States is not a belligerent party."

It took all my effort to sit there in the dark and not beg for answers to my questions. I trusted this LouAnn. She seemed like a professional. I thought we all needed something strong. I poured us coffee with a shot of anisette.

LouAnn said, "I knew that Buddy had died in an air strike, risking his life to ready the ships. I had no idea he had first committed a senseless murder."

All is fair in war, I thought momentarily, as I steeled myself for the worst. But your father's voice got low and weak. "Buddy was brave. He didn't die in the air strike. No. I found Buddy. It wasn't a Jap bomb . . . Our own daisy cutter did him in. Let's leave it at that. We used it to wipe out a fat stripe of jungle fast for landing aircraft; one blast and it'd take anything in its wake. Buddy was sliced lengthwise like an insect. He never had a chance. Never had a chance . . . It was horrible. Finding him like that. His back missing, his insides exposed."

"Okay, that's enough," I stopped him.

"It's okay," LouAnn said. "I'm a nurse—cardiac now. I've seen as bad or worse, I assure you."

I poured us all another generous shot of anisette.

LouAnn said, "I had a miscarriage and didn't write Buddy—he never knew I was pregnant. I didn't see any sense in sending him that bad news. I knew when he came home we'd try again." She gave a sweet little half laugh. "I didn't get on with his family. I never cheated on Buddy. I came here as much to give you this medal 'cause you deserve it, not Buddy, as to tell you that. I know it looked another way back in our day when a woman went certain places alone."

"Una donna sola," I blurted.

"Excuse me?" LouAnn said.

"Oh, it's an old Sicilian saying, means a woman alone is always worrisome—and important."

"Right. Well, I wasn't important. Just weak and lonely. After the loss of the baby, I had no one to talk to. I told Buddy everything but that. I had no idea his family was sending him that crap." Her color changed and she looked furious for a moment, then let it go. She looked around the parlor and saw all the snapshots of the family. "Looks like you got a bunch."

"Ten, one passed away, so nine," I gave her the drill. "Plus let's see, I think we're up to 15 grandkids."

"God bless you both." She smiled big and toasted us. "I wasn't close to Buddy's family. Not like you—Italians."

"Sicilians," your father and I answered at once.

"You take care of each other. I took my maiden name back. I never wanted to remarry. I've had a few long-term boyfriends. I guess I'm meant to be—how'd you say it, a donut solo?"

"Close enough," I smiled.

"I'm gonna leave you two to your girl talk," Vincent said.

When he was gone I asked LouAnn for a cigarette we could share. "If he comes back, it's yours."

"Me, a nurse," she said, "I quit 40 years ago and just bought this pack three days ago after I read the diary." She took out a pack of Salems and lit one up for us to share.

I took a long drag and said, "Why don't you think Buddy deserves the medal? He died serving his country."

"But he also murdered a Japanese prisoner of war." She pointed to the blue-bound manuscript. I said, "I doubt if Buddy was the first or last to . . . you know . . . all is fair in war . . ."

"Not if I have to know about it. From what I've just seen and what he wrote, your husband seems like a fine fellow. I will always wonder what it's like to be married and raise a family for, what, I guess nearly 50 years. I loved the cannoli story . . . Ah, when I read that, I thought if only Buddy had such a way with words. If only he communicated with me . . . I wonder now if maybe he let himself be killed."

"You can't let yourself imagine that."

"Yeah, you're right. It's all so long ago, but ain't it something how words can make it seem like yesterday. Your husband's quite a storyteller."

"It's his saving grace."

"I just had to meet the woman that inspired such prose—the face that launched a thousand words."

"I'm hardly that face or woman anymore."

"Aren't you glad?"

"Yes, come to think of it."

"I was just gonna take a peek at your house, but it looked inviting—all those little kiddie clothes I could see on the line in your backyard."

"Oh, those—my oldest daughter's got a bunch of kids too, and her washer broke. Our dryer's broke. Y know, something's always broke."

LouAnn and me, we made our girl talk about my kids and

grandkids, her nurse work. She told me about her love life and—you girls are old enough to hear this—I have to admit I've always wondered what it would've have been like to be like her, free to come and go and have so much time alone, something so rare for me, and to have had more than one man. Bite my tongue. Someday I'll tell you girls even more about Sicily.

Mom looked around quietly at her daughters. I wondered if she could detect my sisters' silently gleaming eyes. Sometimes not just war, but love, is a long stretch of silence.

Monday, November 4

It seemed as if there was always something new to learn about our parents. After all they come to us fully formed and set in certain ways when we are their infants. Then their pasts begin to slowly unfold backward as we move forward into our futures.

With my father's war diary had surfaced new backstories. Dad's World War II experience took place in Port Moresby, New Guinea, from 1941 until late 1943. Amazing that Mom's new best friend, LouAnn, had had the diary in her attic all these years. A mind-boggling story. More concrete evidence that my parents had lives before mine. I didn't know why Dad would prefer it had been destroyed in the war.

LouAnn and Mom were now thicker than thieves, even closer than Mom had been with her secret pal Francesca, who she'd known in Battin High School, her only unmarried friend. I think Mom's Sicilian vacation prepped her for someone as earthy as LouAnn Harris. LouAnn was a war widow, child-free, who never remarried.

I heard Mom say into the phone that they would head to the Alibi Lounge on Route 1 to have a drink. I knew a smoke was included. Mom had just started and only smoked away from Dad. I was happy for Mom to have girl talk with someone other than her daughters. In some uncanny way, Mom was a war widow too. She says Dad, the man she kissed and sent off to war in December 1941, never came back. I stopped by to see Mom when they were back from mass and Dad had gone off to do some paperwork at his produce stand. I couldn't wait to get the full skinny.

LouAnn had been married to Buddy Higgins from Camden, New Jersey. He was Dad's crew chief in New Guinea and they became good friends. Dad assisted Buddy but they were equals in their minds. Dad had attended Casey Jones aeronautics school and helped in maintaining what he called "our flimsy set of planes." Over the years, Dad had occasionally spoken of his war buddy. "Buddy Higgins was a fine man and an ace soldier," he would say. He'd get sentimental, sometimes tear up.

Buddy was killed in action during a strafing by the Japanese in 1943. We hadn't known the details until now. All the soldiers were encouraged to keep journals—it was believed to help them psychologically. Maybe it's cynical to think, but it likely also helped legitimize the concept of war. Buddy received the Medal of Honor posthumously; it was sent to LouAnn along with the journal she stowed away and did not look at for more than 40 years. A letter from some of Buddy's long-lost relatives in Ireland finally inspired her to read it. A few pages into the 50-page document, she realized it was actually the journal of Vincent Donitella. After that it was easy enough to locate my father.

Dad did not want to read about the war. Mom thought the memory of his friend Buddy being killed opened old wounds. We didn't talk about wounds.

I wondered and wondered how much could be explained about Dad's dark moods, about his yen for ten more children. Mom had not yet read the journal. She said he wanted to burn it but she took it and hid it somewhere. "It's a precious document," she said. She didn't want any of us kids to read it yet. "It was typed on a manual like the V-mail he used to send home, all those bunched-up letters. Someday you kids will need to know more of the truth."

"About what, Mom?"

There was a twinkle in her eyes. "About the Last Cannoli."

What? I didn't push her at that moment. We all knew about the magical cannoli, frozen in time in our freezer. The good luck cannoli. It was an incarnation of the Last Cannoli in the family fairy tale, the one the spirit of Grandpa Donitella snatched from the great beyond. I was more drawn to read the war diary, the war that Dad used to talk about before I was born.

Magdalena and LouAnn are sitting in the dimly lit Alibi Lounge on Route 1 in Rahway, smoking. Between urgent puffs Magdalena tells LouAnn about Sicily and Madeleine.

"Ten?" says LouAnn.

"Last count," says Magdalena with alcohol-induced smugness.

"*Mama mia, how did you do it?*"

Magdalena, still smug, says, "Yeah, me-a-mama. You don't think about how . . . In my situation, you wait for the next one to knock at the door." She knocks at her belly. "And drop in, I mean out."

They both laugh at their silly chatter, then get serious.

"The one . . . you lost . . ." tries LouAnn.

Magdalena serenely replies, "Madeleine, lucky six. She wanted to be a nun, thought she had the calling. She got called all right."

LouAnn thinks of another early death. "Buddy never knew I was pregnant—by him. I lost the baby. But losing a teen must be hard."

Magdalena valiantly waves away the insinuation. "Ah, our religion harps on God's will. But I grieved, then took a solo trip after her death. I went to Sicily and came home liberated, no longer the humble obedient wife. I had done my part, accepting all these bambini, *putting myself last. I stopped dyeing my hair, cut it short and smart, started wearing comfortable shoes, no more make-up. I think I'm more women's libber than my daughters."*

"Bravo! Let's get another round of these," says LouAnn as she points to the empty glasses, "and celebrate libber . . . tee. I never remarried and no regrets."

"Same . . . I mean no regrets. But Vincent, it's like more kids will fill some void. We've switched roles. I wear the pants, complete reversal."

"Waiter!" LouAnn calls. "We're celebrating replete comversal. Two more."

"Two more vodka martinis, coming up," nods the waiter.

Tuesday, November 5

A triumvirate of Catholic churches with schools was home away from home at some point for our family. St. Anthony's in Elizabeth was where my parents and their siblings got married, where they still prayed with the faithful. St. Mary's in Rahway was where the second five of us kids attended grammar school, confessed our sins to a monotoned priest in a darkened wood box every First Friday—after we were initiated to the age of reason through First Holy Communion. Blessed Sacrament, not far from Dad's produce business, was where the first five siblings attended grammar school and were recruited into the faith. It was also where I was student-teaching until my Mother Seton job began in January. The nuns recognized my name and I would listen patiently, even amused, to stories about Mario, Lucy, Carmine, Vinnie, and Frankie, mostly how studious and dutiful the first three were, how mischievous were the last two.

More filling in of blanks before my time.

But this business of my father being blackmailed distracted me from teaching. I couldn't share this with anyone, not my siblings or my mother, not my boyfriend who was away at grad school in California. I didn't know how, but I felt confident I could tackle this problem for Dad. I was truly possessive of this drama. I surprised myself. But it would be my personal firsthand experience. My *memoir.*

Sometimes I would try to get to the produce stand before anyone else. We still called it a stand even though it was now a spiffy new structure with electricity, heat, air-conditioning, two walk-in refrigerators, heavy double doors that slid open easily, and plenty of space, about 1,500 square feet. Awnings shaded outdoor displays of seasonal produce to tempt customers, and a small shed stood at the back for waste and recycling. The original building had always been used by purveyors of Jersey farm food, at least since the Roaring Twenties. Being so close to the railroad, it reportedly housed a bread and soup line during the Great Depression.

I had searched the storage area easily enough, poking into corners, looking for dropout bottoms, secret drawers. I checked the one walk-in refrigerator that wasn't locked. Unless there was a door concealed behind the stacked crates, nothing was hidden in there. I knew for a fact that Sammy meant business and I was pretty sure the watches were around somewhere. I had overheard my parents' conversations in the parlor about *orologi.* After all these years, they still thought we kids didn't understand Sicilian just because we didn't speak the dialect. We might not know exactly what *stunat'* or *porchetta* or *fangool* meant, but we knew when and how to use those words.

Dad was sure the watches had been stashed at the produce stand, maybe during the night. Speaking in rapid Sicilian, he said he couldn't figure out where they might be hidden. "Maybe it's better if I don't know." Even after seven months he still didn't know all the nooks and crannies of his expanded business location.

As for Mom, she took it in stride. Dad's drama, Dad's dreams—she had learned not to get pulled by the undertow. She stopped biting the back of her hand and start using Dad's invectives. "Just tell the ham'n'egger to go pound salt," she said.

"I already have," Dad told her in a weepy voice. "How am I gonna get the mansion with a crime hanging over my head?"

When they went out back to the garden, I opened the freezer door of their black refrigerator. With its brass handles, vertical doors, and small smoky mirrors, it looked more like a coffin. I spotted the Last Cannoli in its bridal veil. I was crystal gazing again through the tiny diamonds of frost. And I saw that despite all obstacles Dad would get his dream this time. *Please, dear Madeleine, help us.*

Three days a week I helped Dad. This morning I arrived early, slowly walked the scrawny field wrapping the market. I wondered if there was a cellar trapdoor hidden in the weeds. But none appeared. The ground was solid as granite. I thought I spotted some old *god-dunes* among the weeds some way from the main building. They were growing around a concrete-block structure about the size of a double outhouse. I didn't recall seeing that before. It must've been added recently. There were milkweed and wild mustard, both edible in a pinch, and some skunk cabbage, poisonous to eat but apparently with homeopathic applications I had not been inclined to test.

Then I noticed a small iron door on the concrete block with a black-and-red danger sign, posted by the city of Elizabeth, indicating it housed electrical wiring. That explained why I hadn't seen it before. Too dangerous to fiddle with. I figured even if the *god-dunes* grew there, they'd be radioactive, tainted by the electromagnetic field too near. I knew sure as Shinola is black that the stolen merchandise was somewhere on the property.

When Dad arrived he went to work quietly. I said, "Dad, remember how you used to tell me the world would end when there was no more Popsicle sticks?" He never actually told me, he only told the others who told me.

I wouldn't bring up the war diary. I heard that Dad once used to talk too much, even in his sleep, about the war— after all, the day after he returned he had to set to work earning a living and raising a family, nuclear style, like others in his generation. Like other war vets he had no transition time, no head space to digest what he had been through. They went from killing fields to serene pastures, rural villages, or quiet suburban neighborhoods, land that had yet to see a modern-day war. Dad had seen horrible death of men he knew intimately, death that time and duties had never allowed him to mourn. Of course the journal was apt to break him open, bring out his dark self.

My father smiled wanly at my question, but didn't answer. He was not in his jokester mood. At least he seemed mildly pleased at the memory. It was a ploy to get his bright, chatty side out, front and center. The day before he had been feeling jocular when we went once again exploring the run-down old Mariners Mansion, the would-be orphanage. A new home for the next ten kids Dad would, well not sire, but take in, give refuge from the cruel world. Save ten, save thousands, I guessed.

He loved his many grandchildren but they were safely on their way to all the opportunity the American dream offered, the dream his father drilled him on until it brought about his untimely death. At least that was how I imagined he saw it. Dad was just 19 when his father died.

I laughed recalling how my father had again scared off the juvenile delinquents who did God knew what in the beat-up, crumbling rooms. He smoked them out with a few cap bombs, harmless but noisy. My father could look scary and official with his six-foot frame, dark eyes, dark hair just graying at the temples, and firm, confident stride. He did not raise his voice, kept it steady and dark.

He pretended to be the owner—as he believed he would be one day. He told them gently, "If you boys don't have parents or guardians to go home to, I'll let you live here once it's renovated." I could tell by the looks on their smudged faces they heard *reform school*. That scared them off for the time being. They backed away quietly and would probably keep away for a while—especially if they saw his car out front. I tried to see his vision beyond the crumbling structure. It had good bones, as I heard him say. But what time and weather and neglect hadn't done, vandals had.

He lifted a crate of radicchio, another new item, Venetian,

pretty as an ivory-and-purple ceramic sculpture. At last he said yes, he remembered something about the Popsicle sticks. But not why he had said it.

We both tended to a stream of customers, mostly old Italians and some of the new immigrants from Latin America, who had inspired us to carry the sudden explosion of unusual fruits and vegetables. It got quiet again and I saw Dad was off brooding, perhaps about Sammy's strong-arming.

"Dad, how does that song you made up about the girl of your dreams go?" Obliging in a mechanical voice, he recited:

The girl of my dreams has bobbed her hair
And dyed it a fiery red
She drinks, she smokes, she tells dirty jokes
She hasn't a brain in her head
The girl of my dreams is a cigarette fiend . . .
And the sweetheart of six other guys.

I clapped. "*Bravissimo*, Dad. How about the Tale of the Last Cannoli. Maybe I'll share it someday with my English class as a model of family mythology in the form of oral tradition. Tell me it again."

He looked bewildered, as if he had never heard of such a story. But he said, "Not now." Then he abruptly stopped what he was doing and focused on two men in the distance, headed up the path to the market. He looked apprehensive. "Not now. I see customers coming."

I turned my gaze toward the men approaching. Both were dressed sharply and formal in suits, ties, white shirts, and expensive leather shoes. As they got closer, I noticed one man, wearing tinted Coke-bottle glasses, had a deep scar on his left cheek.

"Dad! Are those guys auditors or something?

In a suddenly sharp voice he said, "No! Go check on the produce in the walk-in."

"I thought you did."

"I said go. Hurry. Check again."

I backed away slowly, bewildered, as the two men greeted Dad.

HOOD 1: Vinnie, we ran into our mutual buddy Sammy.

HOOD 2: Yeah. He thought we should pay you a friendly visit.

Dad kept staring darkly at them.

HOOD 1: You got a nice upgrade here from the old exposed stand you had, what with all this land, a good acre?

DAD: What do you want? Don't beat around the bush.

HOOD 1: What we want actually has already been achieved. That's all you need to know.

HOOD 2: Yeah. That's all.

They turned to leave but Hood 1 turned around.

HOOD 1: Oh yeah, a tip. Just remember your late great father. How he claimed the barrels in his cellar held only flour.

DAD, lurching forward with balled fists and stopping: You *gavon'*, don't you dare speak my father's name.

HOOD 1, raising his palms to signify, stop, no problem: Vinnie, Vinnie. I come in peace. Just saying it's in your blood to turn a blind eye . . . should you . . . come across . . .

DAD: Hot goods, that what you're going to say?

HOOD 1: Nah. You said it. I was going to say *something surprising . . .*

The men departed with Dad staring daggers after them, hyperventilating, then noisily moving crates. I was standing just inside the front door, out of sight but within earshot. I tried to hide my anxiety and anger. As I stared unnoticed at my father's face he stopped working, stood and stared into the distance with a look of despair. I felt like my namesake, Old Carmela, who could see deep into the past. In my father's mind the present had dissolved to an old-time cellar. He was ten years old again.

Young Vincent is dressed in the attire of the day, black stockings, knickers, newsboy cap. By his side a large calendar pinned to a wooden door shows the year 1930. Vincent's eyes are trained on his father. Mario is in his 40s, short but solidly build, looking solemn and wearing a white butcher's apron.

Mario opens the wooden door to a dark windowless cell where half-light shines on six or seven large wine barrels. He points with an open hand and takes his son into his confidence.

Shrugging his shoulders, Mario says, "They tell me flour. I don't ask."

Young Vincent shakes his head in disbelief. "Pop! Don't smell like flour, smells like moonshine."

As my mind reeled from shock to despair I was filled with determination to help my father.

"Dad, remember you used to say the big things have to happen, it's the small things that bug you."

He shot me a quizzical look. I only knew he said that from my mother and Vinnie, who often quoted my father. "That's right, honey, a good rule of thumb for life . . ." He seemed distracted again.

"I was just wondering. Um . . . Sammy storing those hot watches at your produce business. Is that a big thing or a small thing?" I knew I had hit a nerve but I wanted to gauge how much it worried him.

He hummed "The Girl of My Dreams" again. Silence ensued. So I hummed "Stardust." That got me a dirty look, as if I had cursed before the altar in church. But it wasn't the song that bothered him.

"What watches. What produce," he said, calm as an English cucumber.

I got his drift.

"How much do you have to guarantee to put into renovating the old mansion?"

"About fifty thousand."

"You have a year to do it?"

"Two, I think."

Later as we closed up and left, he said, "Let's stop at St. Anthony's and light a candle before St. Jude and the Blessed Virgin for help with lost causes."

Before we entered the church he answered my dangling question. "Small thing, Cat, small thing." Inside he crossed himself twice. I followed suit.

Wednesday, November 6

The origins of the Sicilian pastry known as cannoli can be traced back to the 10th century during the Arab rule of Sicily. The dessert, believed to have been influenced by the Arab love of sweets, became a popular treat among the wealthy Sicilian nobles. It is still the aristocrat of pastries, Sicilian and otherwise. The traditional cannoli consists of a crispy deep-fried pastry shell with a sweet, creamy filling made from ricotta cheese, sugar, and flavors such as vanilla, chocolate, or candied fruit.

And it is greater than the sum of its parts.

My sisters' eyes remained dark until they spoke. Then their eyes flashed and lit up and glittered in their sockets in the colors my mind had given them. The vision held me in a trance of heightened sensitivity, even as I heard and understood every word they were saying.

Everything I knew about my family was through someone else's eyes. Hearsay that had become dogma, truer than if

I'd been there. My memories were jumbled with everyone else's to the point of delirium if I tried to separate them out. Maybe I *was* there.

Numero Dieci, last born, the baby, 20 years younger than *Numero Uno.* Dad had started to lighten up on his mandatory storytelling sessions by the time I was born. My siblings told me they used to have to crowd into our little parlor every night before supper. They said I was there too as an infant. Their friends were still out in the street playing and they could hear their calls and laughter. But Dad would not budge. He would tell stories mostly about Sicily, where his and Mom's parents came from. All four of my grandparents landed in Peterstown—which remains the Italian enclave in Elizabeth, New Jersey, to this day.

And because Dad's father, Mario Anthony Donitella, worked so hard the American way, he died young, at 50. Dad had still been trying to come to terms with being the son of an immigrant, trying to make Grandpa happy and proud. Grandpa knew my mother, Magdalena Coniglio, because Mom as a teen would help Grandpa with his English for his insurance work. Dad was still in his wild youthful days then.

Lucy, who earned her degree in psychology after the second or third of her four children (maybe she would outdo Mom and Dad), thought that Dad's insistent storytelling was his way of doing penance for various mischiefs in his youth before he settled down to marry, raise a family, and go off to war, *a right and just war.* Instead of the priest's canned penance of three Hail Marys or three Our Fathers, he wove together vivid stories, cinematic in detail, about the island he had yet to set foot on. He recited them like the benediction in a high mass.

Even Maria and Teresa, numbers eight and nine, recalled things I never knew about myself. They were the closest to me in age, five and four years older respectively. They could recite chapter and verse of Dad's old stories about "our people from Agrigento" and how Sicily, *la Bella Sicilia,* was the original Garden of Eden—or of *eatin'*.

Maria told me that when I was two, a bad thing happened to me. Somehow, with all the chaos in our crowded home, boiling water got spilled on my side. From the stove? Or table? I forget. I was scalded with third-degree burns. My baby skin peeled off with my clothes and I spent a week in the hospital being treated so my skin would not get infected. I sometimes searched the affected areas—my left side and arm—for clues. There were none, not even scars. My skin grew back normal. And try as I might, I had no recollection of that trauma.

It is odd how others can recall your pain and grieve for you, actually carry it for you. Maria or Teresa could never tell that long-ago incident without tearing up, as if it had happened to them. They were the only ones to talk to me about it. As if it were a dark family secret kept from me, the subject at the center of it. A wound too terrible to mention.

I wrote a first-person essay about it for an English comp class. Still, I couldn't relate to its being real. Not even a dream. Not even a buried memory.

My sisters said that at the time everyone thought I had died because Mom and Dad came home from the hospital empty-handed, without me. They would not talk about it. It was a big thing.

And so something odd began to happen to me. Because I felt so left out and bereft of our family memory, not even privy to my own, without meaning to I developed a way of seeing, imagining you might say, or imaging. But I swear on Sister Alberta's habit, I really do see things, like the precious-stone eyes of my sisters. It's as if my inherited sense of poetic justice from my father had crossed with my need to have my own memories. If I told anyone, they'd say I was hallucinating: *What are you on?* Or that I had a wild imagination. And I would be fine with their thinking that. After all, Mario, my scientist brother, once told me things only tend to exist. All the world's really a hologram. Well, that was how I heard it.

Grandma Coniglio's railroad flat on Christine Street in Peterstown was like that of Old Carmela, the tea-leaf reader, ripe with old and new country smells, from garlic to Clorox. This was where she once threw a skeleton key down from the second floor at my father, missing his head by a hair's breadth, according to the Tale of the Last Cannoli.

My sisters and I met there and ate caponata with ragged hunks of Grandma's crusty, large-crumb Italian bread and sweet butter. We dipped it in Swiss chard from her garden, swimming in olive oil, and used it to scoop up her roasted peppers. We waited for Grandma to stop saying "*Mangiate, mangiate, nipotine mie,*" and leave us to go sit in front of the TV console that was blasting the soap opera *Search for Tomorrow*. She improved her English that way.

Lucy had driven in from Bradley Beach, Rena from Hoboken, and Maria and Teresa from their shared apartment in Rahway. I was finishing up at Dad's produce stand nearby. They asked about Dean, my boyfriend at grad school in California. I said he was fine and not coming home for Thanksgiving. I didn't tell them that I had asked him not to. I wanted to focus all my attention on my father's dilemma, even if he said he thought it was a small thing.

On a bare platter I laid out the one cannoli I had bought from Bella Palermo a few days ago. My sisters' eyes went back to natural darkness as a rare silence reigned for minutes. I pushed the dish with the cannoli to the center of the oilcloth-covered table. They waited patiently for what the sweet centerpiece was meant to announce. Finally Lucy asked, "What's the occasion?"

"Thanksgiving is weeks away," says Rena.

"To share?" Maria and Teresa said together.

I opened Grandma's silverware drawer and passed over Yvonne, Annette, Cécile, Emilie, and Marie, her tarnished but famous Dionne quintuplet teaspoons. I chuckled imagining us five sisters atop vintage spoons. Instead I put out five of the small demitasse spoons. I thought of a line from a poem I had just read by T.S. Eliot, "I have measured out my life with coffee spoons."

Normal conversation continued and without my saying, we each started picking at the crust and creamy filling, eating it in tiny bits as if it were Holy Communion. *Hmmms* buzzed around the table.

And then, that vision—call it a hallucination if you like—returned. It was too real. I looked around at four pairs of dark eyes, dark hair, all features unmistakably from the same gene pool. In a wink, each of my sisters had eyes that were precious stones, each sister's differently colored. It actually started years ago when I was very young—when I still had five sisters, before Madeleine died. But always the same color came from each sister. I think I was in first grade when Sister Elise told us the world would end on Judgment Day. I wanted to take my sisters with me when the earth split open—along with the jewels I knew we would never have, unless they were embedded in their eye sockets.

Lucy had sapphire-blue eyes. Rena had emerald-green eyes. Maria had golden-topaz eyes. Teresa had red-ruby eyes. Madeleine's eyes had been amethyst-violet.

The eye-stone colors never varied. As if my brain were a mood ring, displaying the color that went with each sister's aura. This vision did not distract me from what we were discussing. In fact, it turbocharged my attention to the matter at hand. When I was old enough to understand the facts of life, I used to imagine that my mother had a different lover for each daughter. I wanted her to be like a woman out of a Renaissance novel. Fanciful eyes, a fanciful thought I would never share with anyone. Oh, and I imagined I had tigereyes that could bore though BS. Like Sammy Bono's.

"Madeleine has been showing up in my dreams," I said casually as I spooned a crushed bit of crust and filling onto my tongue. I left out that she started to appear right before the watch fiasco at the Villa Roma. My sisters didn't react. It was routine dream reporting. We all had vivid dreams and were used to my parents reporting dreams of dead relatives. Dad told a story of his father appearing in a dream and waking him from deep sleep because the flame had gone out on a burner where he was brewing coffee. He'd have been gassed to death without Grandpa's warning. Mom dreamed of Great-Grandma's death days before she passed on in her sleep peacefully at 92. And of course there was Dad's father's role in the Tale of the Last Cannoli. A strain of clairvoyance definitely ran in the gene pool.

Lucy, who liked to interpret symbolism both in dreams and in everyday reality, asked me, "What is Madeleine saying?"

"I don't know yet. Maybe she's trying to tell me something that would have kept her from dying." I was only seven when she died in 1970 at age 16. I didn't recall a lot about it.

Rena chimed in, "She died because she wouldn't go all or even part way." She was not being sacrilegious or disrespectful. Because Rena was closest to Madeleine, she knew that her sister was holding on to her virginity, waiting and waiting for marriage, when all the teen girls around them were testing the sexual waters.

"I suppose," said Lucy, "an aneurysm can occur if one gets too hot and doesn't release the heat."

"You mean because she couldn't have an orgasm *down there* she had an orgasm up there?" Teresa said.

We all laughed. Maria embellished this theory. "Gives new meaning to *wet brain*."

We booed through ghoulish smiles. I said, "It's really too

late for this postmortem." I knew it was all self-serving, something to help us manage the loss, the grief over the years. We could talk about the dead with ease but almost never about the walking wounded. Strangely, it was harder for us than for Mom and Dad, who prayed and moved on. Mom went to Sicily alone to visit her cousins and Dad's for the first time. Dad had still been silently, stoically, pining over his son who came home injured from Vietnam. Another example of Dad's theory that the big things have to happen.

I told my sisters that in her last appearance in my dream, Madeleine was telling me to look deeper into Dad's Tale of the Last Cannoli. Or was it into the Last Cannoli in the freezer?

"Can you believe it? That cannoli is petrified in our freezer—probably defrosted and refrozen how many times since 1941?" I prodded.

An odd spell of silence ensued which I took to be reverence. Suddenly Rena segued, "That's his best story," her eyes glowing emeralds. "A vestige of a bygone time."

"It's got that wonderful fairy-tale scent, that ending," Lucy crooned, and her eyes glimmered sapphire. She took a spoonful of cream from the diminishing pastry.

"Remember when we called them *gah-nole*, not cannoli, like the Americans, the *Merican'*?"

"Yeah. Mom says Sicilians often drop the last syllable and make the C sound like a G."

"We used to say *biscot'*, not biscotti."

"*Mani-gaut'* for manicotti."

"*Gobba-gool'* For capocollo."

"*Mutz* for mozzarella."

"*Ri-gaut'*, not ricotta."

"*Pro-shoot*, not prosciutto."

Maria and Teresa, so close that they often said the same thing at the same time, chorused, "That story is a treasure map of Dad's soul." Their eyes flashed golden and ruby-red respectively.

Lucy-Sapphire again: "Remember Mom's story when she returned from Sicily?"

Yes, we all answered. "Maybe Madeleine is reminding you of that," Rena-Emerald said.

"Like the cannoli symbolizes Sicily?" I asked.

Lucy pondered. "Here's what I think—some guy at the municipal building, after realizing Mom had just lost a young daughter, told her, 'The family treasure is what hides in your heart.' That was after she exhausted him trying to find records that went back to Sicily's Stone Age, along with stories about the ancestors, to find some treasured connection to the present."

"So all you have to do is configure the details that suit your heart's desire?" I said.

No one answered.

Not wanting to fixate on my nighttime dream, I changed the subject. "Dad wants to have ten more kids. That's the real reason I have gathered you here." They knew I sort of joked.

"What are we," asked Lucy, "chopped pâté? He wants to replace us?"

"You mean liver," corrected Rena.

"Same difference," said Maria. "One just has a fancy

French name. *Pâté* means paste. Yuk."

"Is he drinking again?" Lucy asked anxiously.

"No," I lied, not so much to protect the guilty as to keep my sisters on topic. If I said yes, the conversation would take a different turn. We could always address his drinking if it got out of hand. Which I believed it would not. If we could just get the old mansion, fix Dad's finances, get the watches off the property. "Not drinking, not replace us, just expand us."

"Why can't he just house them on Creek Street?" That spurred a rapid-fire chain reaction.

"You kiddin'? You don't remember?"

"One bathroom divided by 12 . . ."

"Equals . . . not a pretty sight."

"Not to mention how we were stacked in beds, like in a warehouse."

"Until we learned to be obnoxious enough to get our own little bedrolls."

"Talk about warehousing kids . . ."

"Oh, c'mon, you all loved it."

"I longed to be an only child."

"In hindsight, sure we loved it because we have the best crowd-pleasing stories of our childhoods."

"Yeah, ten different stories."

"As some wisenheimer said, it's never too late to have a happy childhood."

The banter reminded me of something I had read recently about so-called consensual reality. A writer wrote fiction, stories and novels based on her family. She made up things that never happened. But after her work was published, members of her family believed those events had actually occurred and argued vehemently to the point of great dissension. Even the author couldn't convince the unwittingly duped siblings that she had made up the events in question. The believers told her she was merely recovering a repressed memory. Finally, in order to stay calm and not disown each other, they agreed to disagree. It didn't really matter, they unanimously decided, because neither side could prove what had or hadn't happened. Still they occasionally resurrected the argument and tension flared up.

It was all words and images in their own minds. Memory is always recovered, whether of actual experience or scenes from fiction that are planted somehow in the brain's synapses. I was acutely aware of my own extrasensory skill in hallucinating; I knew I could not always distinguish correctly between real and imagined memory.

That's my story and I'm sticking to it.

Over the years my mother had told us many stories of her childhood that helped flesh out Gemma Coniglio, the woman who was to become our beloved Meatball Grandma.

Gemma and Franco

One day, Gemma heard Franco's footsteps coming up the stairs. It was barely noon, too early for him to be coming home from work. Was he sick? Their eyes met as he came through the door. She saw that he was crying. Franco com-

pensated with softness for Gemma's grittiness.

"The world has good and bad in it and nothing in between," Gemma, who recognized both in an instant, would say. Like with her neighbor, Leonardo Spinello—that Giufà would help himself to a tomato or pepper if she didn't keep an eye out. He couldn't fool her, Gemma Coniglio. She knew every fruit and vegetable her ground put forth. She would stand her hefty body with its sturdy thick ankles on a stool and look down from her second-story window to study the Spinellos' row of vegetables that separated her yard from theirs.

"The boss cut my pay and my hours," Franco told her, as if any wrongdoing were his. It was 1930.

Gemma loved her husband, a man she had vowed to marry even before they met, who brought America down to her size. He knew the big woman God meant her to be. Franco built six-inch-high footstools for every room. Thanks to him, Gemma could reach her arms into all the hidden corners of cupboards and closets in their big, long flat. She may have looked four foot eleven to the world but in the eyes of Franco she reached up to heaven.

Franco unleashed all his tears. Gemma would not have the despair that pervaded the country cross her threshold.

"So the bastardo *cut your pay," she said. Gemma had no compunction about cursing the wicked, which often drove her daughter Magdalena crazy. "Go get a 25-pound sack of flour."*

Franco wiped his tears and looked at her questioningly.

"We'll have macaroni and bread every day, che vuoi?*" She told him to wash up for lunch. They shared a piece of*

sausage, their last meat for a year, and a glass of homemade wine with Franco's mother, Maridona, who lived with them.

Every day for a year, the pastry board and broom handle came out from under the bed. The dust of flour hung in the air. Gemma managed Franco's measly pay well. One day after a year, she bought a half-pound of chopped chuck and fed her husband and three children meatballs fat with cheese, egg, bread crumbs, and fresh mint from her garden.

Three years later, Franco had a job again. He would drink his coffee and descend to the yard before he headed for the factory in New York's garment district where he helped his Jewish boss sew men's suits. Before leaving, he walked slowly along the perimeter where things that he and Gemma had planted were growing, including his seedling peach tree. He had long ago grown to love the square geometry of all the yards on his block, flush with one another, yet with boundaries so clear and defined. As if all the boxy two-family homes and yards came off America's great assembly line. Not at all like the untidy, sprawling mountainous land of the island where he was born. His tailor's mind liked how the vegetable gardens, shrubs, fruit trees, and ornamentals softened the bold straight lines. All fit together like perfectly tight seams.

He salivated as he plucked a snail from the squash plant, then a second and a third. Not as meaty as the cipuddu *in the hills of San Giovanni Gemini. But still good. Later he would drop them in boiling water and slide the chewy meat out with a straight pin. It was still hot and humid in late August. What did he expect? Franco had heard how wet the summers in New Jersey were even before he set sail for*

America. The first years, it meant something extra and luxurious like everything in America, bigger, thicker, fatter. Wetter *rhymed with* better.

But now wet meant wet. Dry meant dry. He recalled the dry frisking of wheat, golden stalk against golden stalk, under golden sun. He checked the memory. The Peterstown sun wasn't intense enough for wheat, but it gave decent grapes, thank God, and even with the hardships of the long Depression, he had his trusty winepress, built with his own hands. No one bothered him or the other winemakers on his block, so long as they let the officers store some barrels of "flour" in their cellars. And he grew good juicy tomatoes and sweet corn. And three "crops" of his own, heh heh, due maschi e una femina. "Your mother, she swallowed two black olive pits and one green olive pit," he told his daughter Magdalena. "That's where you guys come from—olives."

As he eyed the gangly ripe cucuz' from his garden that went into stew every Friday, he thought his only loss was the deep flavors of the Sicilian earth. Franco despaired of tasting ricotta like Sicily's in New Jersey. Even in Peterstown, the milk from the cows was thin, monotonous, and unimaginative. Not like he had in the padrone's farmhouse in San Giovanni Gemini. The difference started in the grass, the grain, the dirt, the clouds—who knew where?—he told Magdalena. And it went on up to the lazy fat cows' udders and nipples. The whole pipeline of equipment was wrong in America. The life force was diminished here, lost in the sheer size of everything. Franco tasted that. He knew what was missing because he could still taste it in memories that wouldn't be buried.

He kept this little complaint like his morning raw egg—

between his lips and God's ear, because he didn't want to get his wife started on her losses. Each day she found more and more wrong. The water company, the iceman, the coal, the butcher, the grocer—all the money the bill collectors were cheating them out of, Madon'. *Franco wondered if she felt bitter about being cheated of more "crops." But he didn't grieve. Who needed more mouths to feed? His complaint was nothing next to Gemma's loss, the harvest of life itself, three short-lived babies. He protected her from his peeves, like the one about how the boss gave him his filthy pants to sew a zipper in, for no extra pay, or how he wouldn't let Franco work with silk. "Your hands are too rough,* Paisan'." *Franco's hands longed to touch and smooth silk. Instead, he made and kneaded the* ciambelle *dough. His* ciambelle *were the best.*

But no matter how much life she lost, that Gemma, she had a lot left in her short, plump body. Franco would never again have life in Sicily, but he had Gemma, her immigration and their marriage arranged by her brothers. That was better because for him plump and firm Gemma was Sicily. He was lucky to have worked with her brothers, who gave her to him. A peach from the tree of life, sweet as the fruit from the tree in his own garden here in Peterstown, the biggest Italian enclave in the world. Gemma was like the cream that yielded the best curds of ricotta and mozzarella he had ever tasted.

And that's what kept Franco going until he died at age 80 of a sudden stroke, with his everlasting quiet smile on his face. Gemma shed more tears than she knew she had and carried on, strong, imperious, irascible. Tough as needed. Tenderest with her granddaughters.

Wednesday Night, November

I woke up in my childhood home on Creek Street knowing I was dreaming. It was not unusual. I knew I was reall sleeping in my own apartment on Roselle Street in Linden, where I had moved only a few months ago. Dad used to say his daughters could not move out of the house on Creek Street until they moved into the protective arms of a husband. But softening came with age. Maria and Teresa paved the way, getting their own apartment in Rahway. I was allowed to move out when I graduated from college.

I was having one of those rare lucid dreams where you are dreamer and wakeful observer at the same time.

Madeleine appeared again, this time full and clear of purpose, and communicative. I could even smell her favorite perfume, Wind Song. At times she hummed the Beatles tune "In My Life." I loved these dreams where all the senses were alive and active. More stimulating than when awake. Or maybe sleep is another form of awake, not recognized yet by our brain's frontal cortex with its highfalutin (as Dad would say) executive functions.

"Forget the guns, take the watches . . . and the cannoli," was the first phrase I could recall, Madeleine playing on that famous line from *The Godfather*. Of course, I'd been worrying nonstop: What should we do about the watches—if we ever found them? Dump them in the river? Sell them for money to help buy the mansion?

Now Madeleine and I held hands and walked through the rooms in our Creek Street home. No one present could see us. Like ghosts of past or future in that Dickens novel. There was a long stretch where Madeleine was telling me about the days right before she crossed over—how Mom used to say it, instead of *died*.

Madeleine

I was just sweet 16, a virgin, and Rena and I were getting in with the in crowd. It put me on the outs with God and the Blessed Virgin. I began to chant "Holy Cannoli," over and over, like an aspiration, to save my soul. I couldn't keep my thoughts pure because of a boy, Freddie, curly black hair and eyes of green. I knew this line of thought was headed toward something I must confess to a priest. One night I slipped—more like poured—my skinny flat-chested body into my burgundy Wranglers and put on make-up, lots of blue eye shadow and black eyeliner. Mom said, "You look like a streetwalker, Madeleine." She sat weary and worn in her rocker in a dark corner of the parlor in those days. Was right around the time when Frankie went to Nam and Dad was in his dark phase. That night, I wanted to bring her closer, to ask her one burning question: How did you and Dad get together without committing sins of impurity? Dad's Tale of the Last Cannoli left out details. But I saw that Mom was only halfway through her rosary. Freddie was waiting at the corner. I said, "Mom, remember we were named after a streetwalker, Mary Magdalene. And look at her, she became a saint, as famous as Jesus."

"Shhhh . . . don't let your father hear you, or we'll have another bonfire in the backyard." Dad had just burned all Rena's and my Beatles cards because John Lennon said the Beatles were more popular than Jesus Christ. I washed off the face paint and changed into my sleeveless mint-green marshmallow-silk dress with a tie around the waist. I pulled my long black hair back with a barrette and met Freddie at the corner of Creek Street. I liked the way he smelled of English Leather. "Wow, you're really dressed to the nines," he said. At first I thought that was something shady and impure. I made a split-second decision to say, "I can't go out, Freddie."

"Why not?"

"My sister just had another baby."

"C'mon, kids are born all the time in your family."

I left him there. In bed I smelled his English Leather on my hand. Despite the horror of pregnancy, I fell asleep thinking about what it meant, going all the way. *It was so strangely relaxing, this thought of going somewhere, and with a boy . . . How could it be a sin? It felt like going for a ride in the country on Sundays, like when Dad was calm and didn't cry or drink too much . . . the chance to have that sort of peace and happiness. But the very thought of it was a sin and I would have to confess to Father Murphy, "Bless me, Father, for I have sinned. I have had impure thoughts . . ." At the thought of having to explain to him that in my thoughts my breasts grew suddenly as big as Marilyn Monroe's or Elizabeth Taylor's, and I had hips and shapely legs, and oh, so much more . . . If matrimony was a sacrament blessed by God, how did he expect you to receive it without having some thoughts about the body? This conundrum bothered me more than what to do about Dad's hot watches bothers you.*

"You gonna wait until you're married to have a date, too?" Freddie asked the next Saturday at the corner of Creek Street. "I'm so sorry, Freddie," I said. "I have to go to a wake tonight and a funeral tomorrow with my parents." It was the truth. Nam had claimed a cousin. This time I gave Frankie my hand voluntarily to kiss.

Rena didn't know that I was sneaking to early mass on Sundays. I couldn't let her or our new friends who smoked and cursed know that I was still hooked on religion. That I believed in God and wanted to keep the Ten Command-ments. I covered my face with my mantilla and hands to pray silently after communion. What came to mind was me and Freddie in his car, driving up to the Watchung Mountains like he wanted to. I was wearing my slinky royal-blue poor-boy dress and my matching royal-blue patent leather sandals . . . and Freddie's arm slipped around my shoulder . . . Then it hit me. I realized that this was a test of my faith. Yes! Sister talked of these tests. To prove that I could pass this test and remain in a state of grace, I must go on a date with Freddie. I was prepared to be tempted to give up my virginity. I knew I would defend it. Holy Cannoli.

Even as I thought this my thighs throbbed and I felt my heart beating in my chest, making my breasts grow with each pulse. I took a cold bath that afternoon and submerged my whole body until I felt purged. "I'm ready to go for a ride up to Watchung," I told Freddie. "Meet me at the corner of Creek Street Saturday." I could hardly eat all week, which did nothing for my hopes of developing breasts, hips, and curves by Saturday night. I could hardly create the soothing fantasies that usually helped me fall asleep. Friday evening, I knew that I had to call it off. I slipped out of bed and knelt before our altar and whispered, "Dear God, I am not ready to take this test. Please save me from my wretched flesh. Dear Mother Mary, save my sister Rena's soul, too. Mary Magdalene, help us all."

Friday night I had this dream: I met Freddie at the corner of Creek where he had been standing for a long time waiting for me. He was casting pebbles into the creek. "To Watchung?" he asked. "Yes," I said. He climbed into his blue Chevy. I slid in on the passenger side and sat next to him. His eyes shone brightly mischievous and green, scary but alluring. Suddenly, it was day and I saw the corner lot was filled with shiny yellow buttercups. I wanted to go pick one and hold it under his chin to see if he liked butter, but he slipped his arm around me and wouldn't let me move. His hand slid down into my slinky blue dress and grabbed my breast that was as big as Marilyn Monroe's. I screamed and pushed him away and ran home. I ran upstairs to my bedroom and tried to wake Rena to ask her how to get a boyfriend without sinning. She was sound asleep and I couldn't wake her. I ran down to the parlor where Mom was rocking and saying her rosary, but she was sad and crying and couldn't hear me. I ran down to the cellar and passed Vinnie, who I knew would listen, but then I saw Mario hanging his head over the piano hitting keys while Carmine studied how they hit the strings inside and made sound. Dad was having a serious talk with Frankie about war and was crying softly. I opened my mouth to tell my father and brothers that this guy had caused me to sin. But I knew they would find him and kill him and that was not what I wanted. Instead I started crying with them because I was so angry that I could not speak. I awoke early on Saturday morning, my head all stuffed up from crying so hard in my sleep. Rena was still sound asleep.

At five to seven on Saturday, I gazed down Creek Street and recognized Freddie's car. He had parked and was looking up and down Creek. He couldn't see me. He waited until 7:15 and then slowly drove off.

That was the night I woke up on the other side, at peace, free of the flesh, free of all sorts of pain, eternally. Holy Cannoli. Carmela Baby, you have no idea!

Madeleine was holding a pastry bag and filling cannoli shells, pointing to the last one. Laughing full-hearted.

When I woke up from this long dream that probably took a couple of minutes to scroll through my mind, I had a few lingering thoughts. Was the hard cannoli shell—tube-shaped, oozing soft luscious cream—a sexual symbol? How about the eternal frozen Last Cannoli the family has kept for years? What was my inner Madeleine trying to tell me—that the watches were not the problem they seemed? How could they not be?

Thursday, November 7

My sisters all knew how Dad used to drool over the Mariners Mansion when it was still inhabited. He thought we could all live there with much more space than we had in our little Cape Cod house in Rahway. He was right but it was just one of his dreams.

"Save ten, save the world," I warbled, not for the first or last time.

"Dream on," said Teresa. She was as glib as the others. They were used to hearing Dad's dreams and stories over the years. But I wanted to believe this was *the one*.

"All we need is one dollar to get the deed," I said. I stood on the optimist's side.

"And a b'jillion within a year," Rena said.

"Or we lose our precious dollar," Lucy said.

Their eyes, blue, green, gold, red . . . And then Madeleine, amethyst-purple, was there, as real as when she appeared to me in dreams.

"Let's go to Caffe Italia for some cappuccino and more

dunking cookies," one of them said. Perfect capping of our meeting for meeting's sake—the only Italian café this side of the Hudson River.

At the café we found a Ouija board. To distract us all I said somewhat capriciously, "Let's ask whether Madeleine is in heaven or hell." Turned out, neither. But we had a hoot of a time struggling to confirm that.

The Last Cannoli was this magical tale my father told from the time before I was born. Of course I knew parts and versions from hearsay. It was said that Dad stopped telling it when our brother Frankie went to Vietnam. War could ignite spells like no other.

But fairy tales had power too. The Last Cannoli was the whimsical story of how my parents were able to get married in spite of Mom's parents' resistance to Dad. It was carved in memories sweeter than pastry cream, stronger than cement. Dad was born with a silver tongue—not in the way of material wealth, something that always seemed to elude him, but in richness with words. Simple words, organic as his fruits and vegetables, homegrown. He could make a poem out of a shopping list. I once heard his a cappella singing as we set up for the day: "The lemons, the limes, the carrots, the celery, the lettuce. Artichokes, cardoons, dandelions, escarole, spinach, chard, broccoli rabe. Fennel in winter. In fall, the cranberries, in spring blueberries, in summer the cherries and watermelon, Chinese apples. Stack 'em up, take 'em down, sell 'em before they go bad. On and on we go in circles that never end, like the children that keep appearing at my table." It was a happy tune that ended with whistling, one of his disposable tunes. He had others that he sang over and over.

Yes, Dad was romantic when he wasn't lost in his own shadows. He would have been a poet, like his father wanted to be too. Words were important to them. Although his vocabulary was not sophisticated, it was colorful and creative. Grandpa Donitella left behind a snippet of a poem that he must have been working on in his Sicilian village.

Grandpa:
The stars peer between trees
Weeping dusty tears upon me

Dad:
Even the rocks, even the wind
Sang a song that rustles through
The soul, forever deep within

Why didn't they finish?

And then there were the silly songs he sang to his grandchildren like:

You're nothing, you're nothing,
You're nothing but a nothing,
A bat is a dumb thing,
At least it's a something

Dad and Mom were the first in our family to speak English like natives of America. My grandparents all spoke broken English, some more so than others. Dad played a word game every Sunday in the Newark *Star-Ledger* that would get him a lot of dough if he ever won. He didn't care if he won, but he was always trying to improve his verbal skills. He was seldom at a loss for words. He even made up words, such as *salsicc' his own*, an Ital-glish play on words that rhymed with *to each his own*. If he was at a loss, it meant something big was on his mind.

Mom told me how Dad had helped his father's cousin Alfonso Tuzzalini and his family make it through Ellis Island back in 1939, when it was still an open gateway for immigrants. The family had passed the physical test, so they didn't need to be quarantined as other relatives had been. But Alfonso was being held on literacy grounds. My father appointed himself legal counsel for Alfonso. He told my mother, "We're still fighting a turn-of-the-century personal vendetta of politicians who want to keep out Italians, Russians, Poles, Hungarians, and other immigrants who don't speak English."

Mom said they had to walk the length of the Great Hall to the front where the Tuzzalinis and the immigration official waited. It was during that walk that Dad proposed to Mom. "He said it so low, sotto voce, that at first I didn't understand. 'Magdalena, would you marry me?' When I didn't answer right away he said, 'I don't like to repeat myself, but I will this once. Would you marry me?' "

Alfonso, his wife, and their two sons were waiting amid a big pile of baskets and baggage that looked as if it had just slid off their backs. My father explained the literacy test to Alfonso in Sicilian. The test looked like a child's puzzle. There were 24 moons with eyes, nose, mouth. The moons were placed six on each of four rows. Alfonso had to find and point to the four moons that were looking to the left, the two that were looking up, and the three that were looking right. He had 15 seconds and he had to begin at the upper left-hand corner and proceed along each line, left to right.

The official was very nice, but he got a little impatient when Dad took so long to explain the quiz. Alfonso took a little longer than 15 seconds because he confused the English words for *left* and *right* a couple times. But the official seemed eager to be done with this, and he allowed the extra time. Then he gave Alfonso some columns of numbers to add up. Alfonso made only one mistake and finally the official said, with no great joy in his voice, "Welcome to America." As they turned to leave, he said to Mom and Dad, "Congratulations on your engagement to be married." They hadn't realized that the Great Hall was a whispering gallery and their voices could be heard yards away.

Maybe the Last Cannoli that was supposed to bring us luck had helped that day and held the key.

Thursday, November 7

For all his verbal skills, I didn't know how Dad was ever going to buy that old mansion. A miracle was needed. I wanted to visit someone who knew more about my father than any of my siblings, who knew the mystical ways of the world.

Old Carmela, my namesake, told Mom every time she was pregnant even before Mom knew, and finally when she was fat with me. When Mom thought nine was a fine round number (as she had thought after four, five, six, seven, and eight), Old Carmela said, "No, you are not done." She lived on Christine Street near where Mom and Dad grew up. Since 1963, when I was born and named for her, Mom and Dad didn't go there so often—maybe in case she told Mom, "You're still not done." But I loved her little apartment and its pantry smell of ripening tomatoes on the sunny sill, garlic braids, dried Italian herbs, boiled coffee, spices, warm olive oil—and Clorox. This afternoon I went there after student-teaching and helping Dad at his produce stand.

Old Carmela was ninety-something. Her vision and hearing were still perfect, though her face was as wrinkled as a dried peach, especially around the eyes. Her eyes were dark with that navy blue tint aged eyes get. For me they flashed on and off golden, the way my sisters' eyes gleamed like precious stones. She wore her hair as she had since her youth, plaited and wrapped around her head. She was quite beautiful in her way.

I would always feel beholden to and kindred with someone who saw me floating in the womb. She welcomed me, Baby Carmela, with an outpouring of Sicilian and a strong hug. She made me sit on a wooden chair at her small enamel table and gave me boiled coffee with lots of milk and sugar and anise-scented *biscot'*. She still sold *god-dunes*, as she had for years. While we chatted she peeled the stringy "nerves" off the cardoon stalks.

"They're almost done for this season," she said.

After I gave her an account of how my siblings and parents were doing, I asked if she had ever heard my father's Tale of the Last Cannoli, the story that commemorated my parents beginning as partners in marriage. She nodded and said the *gah-nole* held memories for those from the old country, even though the pastries were never as good in America as in Sicily. I told her how people always laughed when I mentioned the name of Dad's story. One friend thought the cannoli were a lost tribe of ancient people. And I told Old Carmela that not long ago, when my brother Frankie finally decided to marry his longtime sweetheart, my father told the story again.

I added in a joking way that even though she no longer saw babies in Mom, my father was determined to adopt ten kids, kids who needed a home that he believed he could provide.

"You father wants to start all over? I'm-a not surprise."

"No one is really."

"Tell me this last *gah-nole* story, Baby Carmela."

Old Carmela's cookies were worth their weight in memory. Both my Italian grandmothers had the same recipe. I wish I had known my great-grandmother Maridona—they say she baked cookies like a goddess. Chefs were starting to make *biscot'* for sale commercially, but they could never be the same. Too factory-perfect.

"Okay," I said and started slowly. Old Carmela stared ahead into air and rocked gently like a metronome to my retelling of the old tale. Each time I got to something I thought was deeply symbolic, I'd comment. I noted that in the beginning of the story my father said, "The day I came home to tell my father, who loved Magdalena, that I was going to marry her and pass on his name to many sons, he died. Five minutes before I got there. Angels called and he had to go."

This was my father's first real heartbreak in life. Dad was just 19 and still coming to terms with what his father expected of him. Now he was surrounded by women—his mother and four sisters.

Old Carmela smiled distantly at something, but what, I didn't know.

Next, my father described how he was praying down the Port when his dead father appeared to him over the water.

My mothers' parents didn't think Dad was good enough, rich enough, ambitious enough. Grandpa Donitella's spirit spoke to Dad: *"Do exactly as I say, Vincenzo. Go to Nocera's in Peterstown and ask Gianfranco the owner for a block of the oldest Parmigiano he has. Take it with you when you go to dinner at the Coniglios' this Sunday . . ."*

"But, Pop," Dad interrupted, *"I'm not going to dinner there. They haven't even let me set foot in the house yet!"*

"Shut up and listen to me. Don't think I can't deck you still, figlio mio. *You just do exactly as I tell you. Now, at the dinner you must insist three times that they use your cheese on the macaroni."*

I stopped and looked at Old Carmela. "Fairy tales, parables, myths, all tell us things happen in threes." It did not escape either of us that, even though I wanted to plumb the depths of her wisdom, I was the one deciphering the hidden meaning of the old story. "Carmela," I said, "maybe Dad was really hallucinating." After a moment I told her, the only person I've ever told to this day, that I thought I had inherited his penchant to hallucinate and to believe what I was seeing. After all, she could read tea leaves and coffee grounds.

"*Forse.*" Maybe, was all she could say.

So I continued: how Dad went to Nocera's and asked for the oldest Parmigiano. *Gianfranco winked at him and said, "Aspett', Vinnie, one moment." He disappeared and was gone ten minutes. Returning with a chunk of cheese wrapped in paper, he handed it to Dad and said, "No charge, Vinnie,* curaggiu."

Old Carmela clapped her hands over her breast. "Vinnie, *curaggiu!* Everybody loves you father."

"Yes. Everybody loved my father." Some for the wrong reasons. My father could cast a spell on the most hardened criminal. I thought of Sammy Bono—and yes, Dad could charm him when he was ready to. No matter where we went, Dad pulled strangers into his sphere.

So the story went that Dad, to his surprise, was invited to dinner with Mom's parents. *Dad rang the bell of their second-floor flat on Christine Street. Grandma Coniglio, always known for her toughness, threw a skeleton key out the upstairs window. The large, heavy key Dad would need to get in the door just missed his head. He had passed the first test.*

Old Carmela said, "You grandma Coniglio is a strong-minded woman. Her ways, from hardship of loss of her mother and father. May she pass her toughness on to her granddaughters."

I commented, "Aha, skeleton. Death. Loss of loved ones. Dad was still grieving his father's sudden death." I thought of how Grandma Coniglio had lost two or three babies in the womb before she delivered Mom and her two brothers. Grandma didn't grieve openly. Women lost babies all the time.

So Dad almost forgot until something tapped his shoulder and he remembered to insist three times that Franco and Gemma use the smelly Parmigiano he brought them. As they grated the cheese over the pasta, it turned to flecks of pure gold and everyone was lost in a trance. Dad and his future wife went to the front room and danced to "Stardust." A full moon sent a shaft of silver light through the window and it followed them wherever they danced.

"And that's how Mom's parents consented to her marriage to Dad," I finished.

Old Carmela smiled, sipped coffee, dipped *biscot'*, and nodded. She hummed a few notes of "Eh Cumpari."

I jumped back in. "Now, the gold, the glitter, something bigger and eternal. The alchemy of love, a power to change lead into gold. Additionally, the silver moonbeams and 'Stardust' suggest a romantic and magical atmosphere, further emphasizing the power of love in the family mythology."

Old Carmela spoke at last. "An ancient power, older than dirt, older than God. You father—and you mother—had it." She said it as if they had a pet dog or cat, or a degree in some life science.

"My favorite part," I told her, "is when Grandpa Donitella, his spirit watching Mom and Dad, snatches and eats the Last Cannoli! Grandma Coniglio blamed Dad. But Dad always says, 'I know it was Pop.' "

One more thing I wanted to deconstruct. "Now, the smelliness of the cheese. It is currently conventional wisdom that one must cross and negotiate smelly situations. Smelliness could equal the old, dying, decomposing, the cyclical reality of death and life. The carbon and nitrogen cycles. Without one there cannot be the other." I knew I was going beyond Old Carmela's references. I had heard a lot of the old Italians say, "What goes around comes around," so I said it.

Old Carmela repeated it in Italian: *"Ciò che va in giro viene in giro."*

"What to make of a father who tells stories like that?"

Old Carmela said nothing for a good five minutes. Then she spoke. "We move too fast. We need to listen to stories like that—from the heart—feel and listen to our heartbeat, the beat of the earth. Earth's pulse speeds up, when things are off balance, chaos reigns."

In Sicilian she said, and I understood, "Tornadoes, earthquakes, hurricanes, tsunamis, storms."

I drained my coffee cup and got ready to take leave of the oldest woman I knew, without telling her the sequel to the Last Cannoli that Mom and I had conjured. Old Carmela had provided the perfect sounding board, listening raptly. I realized that the act of telling the story, not just its details, had tremendous power in and of itself, richer than gold, richer than the most precious jewels. Not many walking the earth today can turn something ordinary into something precious. Many do the opposite.

Vincent's Creation Myth

In the beginning, there was terrible darkness. Light, love, and all things good lay frozen in ice. Ice as hard as a stale biscot', as still and cold as Great-Grandpa's breath the day we buried him. But then a sun was born to the universe and a pulse began to beat deep in the earth. When the heat warmed the earth and the buried heart began to twitch, the salt of the earth began to eat the ice. When these things came to pass there flowed over the earth all the great green and blue waters of the world, our oceans, seas, rivers, and streams. And of these great waters of life, none was bluer or more beautiful than one that flowed near the warm half of the world. It was called Mediterranean. For this warm sea was like a plate of church glass, a mirror for the sun.

Now, in addition to love and goodness, many things were freed as the ice melted: gloves, hairbrushes, teething rings, old teeth, old bones, fossils, old sweatshirts, and a dancing hat and boot.

When the sleepy tricornered hat and the boot awoke, they had so much rhythm and happiness and soul that they began to dance together. The hat was all heart and the boot was all soul. They danced and danced together, floating around the world until they were absolutely danced out.

Guess where they came to rest.

They lay down in the Mediterranean Sea. The boot came to be called the Land of Italy and the hat the Land of Sicily.

And then came the mountains of Italy and Sicily.

Now, Italy was nice.

Ah, but Sicilia! Sicily was the most spectacular place on earth. Its coast was blessed with warm sandy beaches and rocky bluffs. Tongues of sapphire water lapped at the sweet, pure land and the sun poured warm gold over the rugged red cliffs. For Sicily was the most wild and free, with a spirit so full of music and rhythm, even the rocks, even the wind sang!

Even the rocks, even the wind.

Every time we visited Grandma Coniglio, her body seemed to be shrinking, in width and in height. She no longer fit her affectionate nickname of Meatball Grandma. Soon her head would be even with my breastbone. But Grandma didn't lose
an ounce in the magnitude of her fussy-woman, ironfisted, imperious nature. Her black eyes scanned sharp as laser beams through all environs, eyes as dark and domineering as my father's. Hence their perennial clashing and adversarial in-law relationship. Underneath their skirmishes I knew they lovedand respected each other. At least, they recognized their own irascibility in each other.

Friday, November 8

February 1942

So this is war. We just dropped two depth charges over the Maui's port side. Practice, not the real thing yet. Boys at play. We boarded the Maui in Frisco. For two weeks sky and water. Lincoln's birthday came. Washington's birthday came, just another day of sky and water. We crossed the equator another day. I was so hot just sitting still, playing cards. A soldier died on board—a draftee who had a wife. We passed an island of Samoa. It was gray and raining. We crossed the international date line. In the doldrums. Waiting to get to war.

I found Dad's journal exactly where I knew it would be, hidden under Mom's wedding gown in her cedar chest on Creek Street. It was a peephole into my father's passage from restless young man to wide-eyed, solemn soldier. It was a crossing, a transformative time no words could fully express. But from where I sat it imparted a deep understanding words alone could never convey. The opening entry portrayed a young man just beyond puberty, bored, waiting for real war action. In a few pages that all changed.

We're short on everything. Our men have never been trained for jungle operations. Chrissakes, there was no time. Some of us have forty-fives, some of us tommy guns, some of us old rifles from World War I. General MacArthur arrived yesterday. The newspaper told us about his arrival in Australia and how the people here think he's a god of some kind. They are pretty sure that America will take Australia after the war and they would love that. They hate the British.

I found myself rushing past the horrors, entered in short but graphic detail—one brave pilot who managed to land and save his damaged plane, even though his arm was hanging by a thread. There was even worse, which I spared myself. I was eager to read more about Dad's much admired friend Buddy Higgins.

Buddy wishes he made LouAnn pregnant—that's his wife. Like me, he married months before he shipped. He's not a whiner. If he dies, it'll be boots on, guarantee. Went to chow and was about half done eating when, wheeee, over come four Zeros and they start strafing again. The raid kept us up to the slit trenches on the hill until 7 p.m. Hiding in a slit trench for hours works your mind in funny ways. I'll know the folds to the Owen Stanley range by heart. I spend a lot of time staring at those mountains for a sign.

Dad wrote about how soldiers milled around when the mail arrived, acting nonchalant about whether or not there was a letter from home for them. He wrote about soldiers getting pissed off for not getting a promotion they felt they deserved, about everyone pissed off at MacArthur. He wrote about how brave and awesome the Aussies were, even when they debated the Americans about whose presence in the war was stronger. They all got drunk one night on some potato-peel moonshine. Finally, more entries on Buddy. Someone in his family wrote that Buddy's wife LouAnn was a runaround. Dad wrote that it was wrong for anyone to send bad news, true or not, to Buddy.

Other night, nearly a full moon, we were expecting Tojo to take advantage of the light, start strafing. We were keeping watch. Some of us were sitting around in our underwear trying to down some K-rations with one hand, waving away the flies with the other. Buddy had such a sad look in his eyes—and it wasn't because of the guy from our squadron whose head was bashed to bits today riding on the running board of a truck that got sideswiped by another one (bury him tomorrow).

Bud wanted to know, "How did you know she was the one?"

"A song," I told him. "We shared a song and it was like that melody was written with our heartstrings."

"Yeah? That stuff really happens?"

"You bet, brother." I saw it made him feel good.

"What song?" Buddy wanted to know.

" 'Stardust.' "

"Ah, Vincent, that's a nice number." Next thing you know we were both humming it. Not another sound around— sometimes war is a long stretch of silence. Then Buddy got to bawling over his wife. Me, I was tearing up. I swear, two saps. I hugged him.

"I know I make a lousy wife," I said.

"You can say that again."

"But you gotta getta grip."

I was astonished by what Dad told Buddy next.

The mood was good. So right here in the jungle, I told Buddy the Tale of the Last Cannoli. In case I never get to tell my wife or our kids. I told him how my future in-laws had to be persuaded that I wasn't a ne'er-do-well knucklehead, so I brought the smelly but magic cheese to their home one night I was invited to supper. My father who died just before I went in the Army Air Corps came to me in a dream and orchestrated the whole thing. I'll skip the details and just say as they grated the stinking cheese over the steaming macaroni, that cheese, it turned to a lump of gold and shiny flakes fell upon the pasta. My father from his grave worked the miracle. The room filled with a golden light and my future wife and me, we went and danced to "Stardust." We both heard it. The moon wasn't silver that night. It was golden and it shone its light on me and Magdalena.

"You know, Vinnie, you got a way with words. I gotta say that." Buddy was enchanted.

"Oh, forgot the last part—my father's spirit was there watching over, so what's he do but eat the last cannoli. Magdalena's folks blamed it on me. I know it was Pop."

"If a person could win this war with words alone, it would be you."

The young man who wrote those words, younger than I was at the moment of reading them, had something in him I would never see. Only my mother knew Dad before and after. Something so astounding, that tale he would tell again and again. The injury dismissed so he would not get sent home . . . the misplaced war honors.

Friday Evening, November 8

In my holographic memory, the one shaped by my siblings, I saw Vinnie, age ten, up on his stilts. I would be born seven years later. Eight-year-old Carmine walked around bent over a magnifying glass with another one in his mouth, studying the rules of the universe. Then the scene shifted to number one son Mario at 17, playing a boogie-woogie on the old upright in the cellar while Frankie swing danced with Dana, our next-door neighbor. Everyone said Dana wanted to marry Mario but settled for Vinnie—and for being Mario's sister-in-law. It was all hand-me-down information and another vision of my siblings that came from what I'd been told—with the occasional rumpled black-and-white snapshot to verify.

The vision faded, except for the piano playing, and I was down the cellar at Mom and Dad's. Mario, now a physics professor at Rutgers, loved to kick back from his intense university job by playing the old piano on Pizza Fridays. Dana, who had long been like one of the guys, was playing gin rummy with the other three brothers on a small card table in the short part of the L-shaped cellar. Rena said when she was a kid Frankie and Carmine used to say, "Sure, you can play cards with us." Then it was either Fifty-two Pickup—she had to pick up the tossed cards—or Knuckles, where she'd have to pick a card and they'd get to strike her knuckles, softly if she picked a black card, hard enough to hurt if she picked a red card. Somehow she always got red.

The cellar, the coolest spot in summer, was the warmest in winter, especially with the oven heated. I found Mom and Dad in the long part of the L, rolling out the dough for many pizza pies. Mom was presiding as Dad followed her instructions. "Not too thin, not too thick, patch that hole." Everyone loved how he deferred to her more and more, new roles for both of them now in their 60s.

Usually they made at least a dozen thick, rectangular pies. We ate the leftover cold pizza Saturday morning for breakfast. Some of the neighborhood kids knew that any Friday of the month might be pizza night at the Donitellas' on Creek Street. They would knock on the door with some pretext, knowing they'd be invited in to eat with us.

Lucy always used to help make the pizza dough before she got married. She loved the magic and mystery of the whole process. She told me more than once, as if she were a high priestess of pizza making, "Leaven is so fragile, without it chaos reigns. Proofing yeast for pizza can be as tricky as trying to harness chaos, especially if a thunderstorm is brewing. On the one hand storm winds might make the yeast lazy. On the other hand, the steamy air could make it *pazzo* and overactive. We always test the temperature of the proofing water on the inside of our wrist, where we test milk for babies' bottles. We add a little extra salt to the pile of flour, not just for flavor, but to inhibit runaway growth. Salt is good discipline for the yeast. Salt helps yeast balance itself between death and too much life. But the most important ingredient is faith. If all else fails, all we have to do is believe in the yeast and it will rise up like Lazarus."

I asked Mom to let me bless the dough as I did when I was a child. I cut a cross into one mound and she said, "*S'benedica.*" The smell of dough and cooking gravy (sauce if you're not a Jersey Ital) filled the cellar with a heady aroma and it was as if that aroma held all the memories and moments from before I was born. I spotted Carmine pouring Grandpa Coniglio's red wine from a big jug into a small squat glass. We called the wine *Centanni* now, only since Grandpa died a few years ago. Grandpa was gone but we still had some of his wine left.

Carmine had just moved back east after several years in Arizona. Rena told me that Carmine, still studying the universe from our planet up to the stars and out to other galaxies, had taken to the hot winds, brilliant sun, and electromagnetic fields of the red rocks in Arizona, the so-called vortexes. He curated Music Traps, a museum of contraptions, where he and others with his sixth sense turned stuff from rummage sales and the Salvation Army into various creations that captured sound. When he was very young he figured out a way to make a teakettle whistle "Stardust" for Mom and Dad's anniversary.

Now Carmine was going into business in New Jersey creating all sorts of fancy, sophisticated music boxes and devices.

He loved music, which he said was older than time mathematics. But he was still hard-pressed to dance. He used to say, "I have to go study the way Dana and Vinnie dance. The way she spirals reminds me of the Fibonacci sequence and I want to plot her coordinates and see if I can learn through that." Now he said he had learned that math, elegant and high-toned as it could be, was the cold-blooded translation of the universe. Music was the warm blood, the plasma, the red and white cells. That was why music alone could bleed every emotion, high, low, and in between.

"How's it feel to be back on flat earth?" I asked him.

"Once a flatlander, always a flatlander," he said, sipping the bloodred wine. He made a face.

"Has it held up?"

He handed me his glass and I took a sip. "Hmmm, I divine the crafty hand of Gramps, wherever he is. When this is gone, we'll never have the likes of it again. What thick body. Almost brandy."

"Yeah, it's special high-test, oughta offer it to the church for sacred liturgy."

"Oh, no, that would be a waste of good grapes." I made a cross in the air over his glass with my left hand and said, "This is *our* blood!"

"Hey, watch that sacrilegious stuff."

"What sacrilege, it is our blood."

"Hmph. Gramps said something similar . . . He used to let me help make the wine. This might be from a batch I had a hand in."

"Tell me."

"It was one day—you were just an infant. We had to go live with Grandma and Grandpa Coniglio while our home on Creek Street was being repaired after the explosion."

Another holographic memory, another wound no one talked about. Everybody knew the explosion had occurred one summer thanks to Frankie, who sneaked down the cellar and played with chemicals in Mario's chemistry lab. He left them out in a sunny window and later, *boom!* Fortunately no one was home. Most of the family were down the shore. No one ever outright blamed Frankie. It was just common knowledge, another unspoken piece of the past.

"Frankie was a real jean buster, wasn't he?" I prodded.

"He was the ultimate till he came back from Nam. But I think it was Vinnie who was the proudest jean buster. He'd go around saying, 'Ma, I wanna be a jean buster too.' He thought it was something cool like being a broncobuster."

I laughed and grabbed a glass. "Pour me some of the precious elixir of Gramps." The wine was like truth serum. Carmine began to tell me a story about Gramps he said no one else knew. Swore me to secrecy. With Mario's piano playing and the others chatting away, no one could hear us.

Carmine and Gramps

I was just about 14 when I began helping Grandpa Coniglio repair Grandma's old wringer washing machine. Next thing I knew I was helping Grandpa make the wine, something no one else was ever allowed to do. Grandpa told me, "I had to wait till you understand that the wine is a living thing. Not just a grape juice." So I asked, "Does it have a soul?"

"Madon', mama mia, what a soul she have! Only you grandma have bigger one." Grandpa said he made the best wine because he understood his fussy woman, Grandma. "Carmine the vine fusses, that's why she give such a good balance of sweet and sour. No pleasure is greater, eh? We need more fussy women, si?"

"Si, si, Gramps, if you say."

Grandpa made me wash my hands and told me to take off my thick-lensed glasses.

"I can't, Grandpa, I need them to see clearly."

"C'mon, you no need. They getta splash."

"I do, Gramps, I don't want to miss anything." I resisted using my magnifying glass.

"Ah, managgia-la, nipote mio. Okay, I had a testa dura when I was young, too."

"Call me whatever you want, but let me keep them on."

I was mesmerized watching the spikes remove the grape stems. The partially crushed grapes fell through the bottom into a deeper basin. The juice bled through the broken skins.

"Grandpa, how brilliant whoever invented the winepress!" I always found out how things mechanical worked. I had X-ray vision for that.

"Si, si, but what's-a more brilliant is what God invented, Carmine, the yeast on the skins that turn the juice to wine in a few days. The press is like-a the wheel. But the yeast is old as God."

Hearing the grapes burst, the juice swish, was when I got my first inkling that music was everywhere in the universe, only waiting to be pulled forward.

As we turned the cylinder crank Grandpa spoke like a high priest of winemaking and I listened. "In Sicily the grain grow everywhere, in the mountain, by the sea, on flat land or on the hillside. But the grapevine is different. The vine is a fussy woman. She only bears fruit on the flat ground. E, si, she like a struggle, so some rock is good. But what she need is lots of sun and some water trickling down her breast. In Sicily, we were so poor. But we always cultivate wine. The grain and the olive is important. But the wine is our blood, Carmine. Not just like in the Bible. We eat a little less bread is okay or even sacrifice a gallon of oil. But we always gotta have some wine with supper."

I interrupted and said, "Carmine, that's a nice-a memory of Gramps but I don't see why you want to keep it so secret."

"I'm-a getting there. *Pazienza.*"

"Okay, pour me a couple more fingers of the *vino veritas.*"

So whenever I was helping Gramps down his cellar he would vanish into one of three stalls. One was storage, one was where the coal for heating was poured in through a ground-level window. And one, where he said he kept fermenting wine, was always locked. He told me kids couldn't go in because the fumes would make them faint.

But one day after we had worked together for a while, Grandpa stood at the one locked stall. To my surprise he said, "You go in first. Alone." I lifted the lock off the door and grabbed the doorknob and opened slowly, hoping I wouldn't faint. I walked inside and my eyes adjusted slowly to the dim light. There was no wine, just some tools, and nothing else but women. On all four walls, floor to ceiling. All of them were naked or seminaked. Two of the walls were covered with old calendars and two walls were pasted all over with color photographs of women from magazines. The women were posing on chairs, benches, sofas, beds, beaches. Some wore just net stockings and garter belts, or feathers and high heels. They had large bosoms. They all seemed to be looking at me and Grandpa.

"Take-a you pick, Carmine."

I looked around for a long time and finally unhooked the calendar closest to me from the wall. It was from 1957.

"That's Christina—she never gets old, eh? You choose her?"

I stared around and around at all the women, blonds, brunettes, redheads, all posing for Grandpa and me. "I guess so. Christina." I took the calendar off the wall and rolled it up.

"You still have her?" I asked.

"Somewhere. I think of her as an heirloom now."

"A collector's item someday . . . No wonder Grandpa always had that Cheshire grin, no matter what he was doing." I thought about what Gramps said about fussy women. "Mom sure did not marry her father. Back when he was young, Dad wouldn't have had a strong-minded woman like Grandma, who always got his ire up."

"Times are a-changing. I think Mom is getting fussy and strong-minded in her old age."

"You noticed? So have the rest of us. Been happening slowly, ever since she got back from Sicily." I decided against telling Carmine about the war diary. And definitely not that Dad might be drinking again. For my brothers, well, they had heard enough about Dad's wartime when they were growing up. Nor would I say a word about the hot merchandise stowed somewhere at the produce business— my brothers would do more than just lean on Sammy Bono and I didn't think that would be a good idea just yet. But I wanted to mention Dad's latest dream.

"You know Dad wants to adopt ten more children."

"More power to him." Like everyone else, Carmine thought it was just another pipe dream.

"He's serious." I didn't know from Dad's other pipe dreams. I arrived on the scene too late. "He wants to buy the abandoned Mariners Mansion down the Port for a buck—that's where he'll house them. He'd have to sell his soul to get the funds to do the mandatory renovation."

"There's always a catch. Sell his soul or his sanity . . . The buck is the devil's carrot."

More than you know, I thought, wondering where those hot watches could be stored. If I was honest with myself, the truth was I couldn't stop thinking about the hidden watches and how much they might be worth. If I could find them. Ah, but I'd be an accomplice to a crime. Could I be an accomplice if I was not in on the original crime?

Sure, I was busting to tell my brothers and sic them on Sammy, the *bastardo*, or as my father would say, the *gavon'*, whatever that means. But I had a plan that I knew only my sisters would go along with.

Suddenly footsteps thundered on the stairs as Lucy, Rena, Maria, and Teresa arrived with young kids running down to the cellar. After the kids came Frankie, limping down one step at a time with his cane.

I heard Frankie yelling over their voices, "Easy, kids! You'll fall, break a neck, and end up like me."

"Oh no, Uncle Frank! We won't go to war."

Another child's voice: "I want a piece with no crust."

Frankie mocked his niece in a squeaky voice, "I want no crust Grammie!"

Other kids shouted out instructions: "Cut mine in strips." "I want extra *mutz*."

Mario was finishing up on piano with "Blue Moon." Frankie, heading to a chair, started singing loud over the chaos. Soon other voices joined in the family anthem.

We are the Donitellas
You've heard so much about
People stop and stare at us
Whenever we go out . . .

There was a time when Dad would order all ten of us to line up and sing it to company. We were so embarrassed. Now we own it and volunteer, nostalgic for our youth.

Donitellas, spouses, and kids, about two dozen of us in all, squeezed around long tables, heads bowed, hands folded on the table. Dad sat at the head, Mom to his right as we all said grace too fast to hear clearly. And speedily blessed ourselves before breaking into conversation. Laughter erupted in spurts, the noise level high and chaotic. Friday night pizza drowned out my worries.

Mom started cutting the thick pies with heavy-duty shears. The pizza in long rectangular trays kept appearing as if Mom's little oven could spit them out on demand, like the magic in a fairy tale where all you have to do is say a few words and out they come by the dozens and dozens. Like the tale where smelly cheese turns to pure gold. And like the miracle of the loaves and the fishes, there would always be leftover pizza for Saturday morning breakfast, however big the crowd around our table.

Saturday, November 9

After coffee and cold pizza this morning at Mom and Dad's I stopped by Dana's old home next door, where she and Vinnie were cooking dinner for friends. Dana's parents had moved to Miami and left her the white-and-red-trim wooden house. It remained uninhabited except when she and Vinnie came back from the flat in SoHo where they lived and taught dancing. The flat was a dance lover's cave of sprung hardwood floors (dancers seemed to float on it), mirrors, quadraphonic sound, and great acoustics. Posters of Fred and Ginger, Rita Hayworth, Gene Nelson, Gene Kelly, and other dance legends lined the walls. They had so many clients in Manhattan, they had to keep a waiting list. Rahway was a fast train ride away from Manhattan but a galaxy distant from Vinnie and Dana's life there.

They had been asking Dad and Mom to show them some 1940s dance steps for a new vintage dance series they planned to offer their students. Before they were married Dad and Mom used to go dancing in Manhattan—the

Apollo, the Cotton Club, the Alhambra, and other places in Harlem. Dad loved that one of his sons chose dance over everything. "You can't *not* smile when you dance," he always said.

"Show me what they taught you," I asked Dana.

"Okay, kid. C'mon Vin." She put a CD of some 1940s music on their new boom box. Vinnie put down his wooden spoon and took off his apron. "Watch closely now."

As Vinnie and Dana swung around he yelled out the various moves. "Here comes the Peabody, the Suzie Q, the Lindy Hop, the Balboa, the swing out, collegiate shag, Big Apple, and the Mickey Rooney, Judy Garland. Watch this syncopated move—*wheeee!* And here comes the Shorty George from Rita and Fred. Here comes our little aerial, and finally, a *sentada.*"

With great airborne poise Dana lifted both legs in a fan and landed on Vinnie's bent knee.

I clapped and asked Dana, "Did my dad remind you how your music won't last like his does?"

"Does the sun rise in the east? Only now your mom has a comeback, tells him he's repeating himself, can't he find a new rant."

"Don't you love the new Magdalena?"

"About time."

No one had missed her change.

Vinnie and Dana went back to food prep. Dana finished hand cranking the fettucine and placed the noodles on a white bedsheet to dry out. The gravy was simmering.

"Sausage detail!" Vinnie yelled.

"Aye aye, el Chef, I'm on it." Dana held the casing as

Vinnie fed the marinated pork shoulder and butt into the grinder. It was Dad's recipe embellished by Vinnie with a blend of fresh herbs. More food magic: Out came long, fat links of Sicilian sausage. The meatballs and stuffed artichokes were done.

I said, "I see Dad got you the chokes from his friend Angelo. They're almost impossible to find this time of year, but these look good and meaty, not like that new spine-free hybrid."

"Sheesh," Vinnie said as he tamped down the pork meat. "You gotta grow your own produce these days if you want it to keep the taste you know and love."

"Dad talks about planting some things in the land around his stand," I said. *If he doesn't have to consult with Bono*, I thought.

"Dana, put the *salsiccia* in the fridge, I'm gonna start on the braciola."

"Tell me how you make the *braciol'*," I said.

Vinnie pounded the flank steak with a wooden mallet until it was a half-inch thick. "You spread the meat with a few tablespoons olive oil, arrange the Parm, egg, *prosciut'*, herbs, garlic, salt, and pepper evenly over the meat."

Dana said, "Let me roll the meat." As the daughter of one of the WASP families on our block, Dana loved showing us how she had been transformed into an authentic *sposa Siciliana*. My father had even changed her name to MaDona. "Watch, you roll the meat jelly-roll style, lengthwise, *va bene?*"

"*Si, va bene,*" I smiled.

I watched Dana's perfectly manicured hands, not a typical

Italian mama's, working confidently. "You secure the roll tightly with string."

Vinnie had the olive oil ready and heated in a skillet. Dana placed the rolls in the hot oil. "You brown the roll on all sides."

When the rolls were removed, she sliced them into two or three lengths and plunked them into the simmering gravy.

"Allow to cook through, leaving the braciola in the gravy a long time—it'll get nice and tender."

Maria and Teresa came over from next door just as the last roll went into the sauce. They told how they nearly got arrested at an Italian restaurant in Newark for sending back braciola that tasted nothing like what our family made. They thought the meat might have been bad—it smelled like old tobacco. The owner, a woman with a voice like the Godfather with a sore throat, accused them of not wanting to pay. She called the cops, who ordered my sisters and their dates outside. Then the cops laughed and said they got a call from the old lady at least once a week. "We would never even think of eating there or stepping foot in the place—we don't want to deal with her. You want a good braciola, go over to Enrico's Café on Magazine Street in Ironbound."

As I sat at the kitchen table watching Dana and Vinnie cook, my holographic memory kicked in again.

The Amazing Vinnie

When Vinnie was about ten he transformed the backyard into a stage and put on his Amazing Vinnie show for the younger siblings and neighborhood kids. Appearing to cut off his fingers, he'd make them disappear and then magically reattach them, a trick that impressed the little children.

"How did you do that, Vinnie?" Rena asked.

"Tell us!" said Maria and Teresa. "Where's the blood?"

"A true magician never ever explains his tricks," Vinnie smiled.

"Do giant-midget," begged Maria and Teresa.

Vinnie, wearing a long coat, walked around on the wooden stilts that Carmine had made for him.. Then, still in the coat, he slid around on his knees that were stuck into shoes too big for him. He had salvaged the costumes from a bin in the cellar where my mother stored all the used clothing neighbors gave to us. Vinnie could enjoy himself entertaining the little kids all summer long like this. He taught them to dance. He was always coming up with new tricks and jokes for them. From behind a sheet or old bedspread hung over the clothesline, he would come on stage announcing, "Ladies and gentlemen and children of all ages, introducing the greatest show on earth and all of Creek Street, Amazing Vinnie!"

Vinnie used to ask my mother, "Ma, can I marry you when I get older?"

"Of course not, you won't want to."

"Mom, I will. I got you on a pedestal."

"Okay, Vinnie, you don't have to repeat everything you hear your father say."

"I love you more than life itself."

"Your name is Vincent all right."

Vinnie would stand below Dana's bedroom window and

yell up how he loved to dance with her.

"Ma, you know what I'm thinking—that Dana and me should go on American Bandstand *and win that dance contest. You'll be proud of me. I know we dance better than any of those* chooches.*"*

"You probably do," she said. "But you have to wait until you're 16 to take the train alone to Philadelphia."

"And convince Dana to go with me. How much older do I have to be before Dana will forget Mario and find me more interesting?"

She laughed and said, "Vinnie, even in eight years when you're 18, Dana will still be six years older than you."

"So what. I want to win her away from Mario. If I can't marry you, I'll marry Dana. I'll win her hand, Mom, the way Dad won yours."

"Where'd you get that one from?"

"Tell me how. Please. Mom, did a lanimated photo of you in Dad's pocket over his heart really make a bullet bounce off him? Or is that just a story?"

She smiled so pretty for Vinnie, just like in her wedding photo, he thought. "Lam-i-nated. Does it matter, Vinnie? What matters is he's here, which is why you're here."

I came back to present time. "Hey, you making *gah-nole* for dessert?"

Dana had already prepared the cannoli shells days before. I knew how to make them but I tested her. "What's the recipe?"

"Three cups unbleached flour, tablespoon sugar, half teaspoon cinnamon, three-quarters cup red wine."

"How about the filling?" Non-Italians were only just starting to enjoy cannoli. Some still confused it with cannelloni, the pasta. Others, like my friend, thought it was a mythical race of people. Most home cooks followed the easier ricotta–whipped cream recipe. But my family favored the classic Bella Palermo mixture made with cornstarch pudding, ricotta, chocolate, and of course almonds.

"Bravo! You pass the test."

"You rascal." Her cropped black hair was naturally pouffy and bouffant, her mascara, eyeliner, lipstick always perfectly applied. Slim and petite, light on her feet, Dana was a confection in herself.

Bella Palermo–style Cannoli Filling

Mix together:
¼ cup cornstarch
½ cup sugar
2¼ cups milk
1 teaspoon vanilla
Cook in a double boiler until thick, about 15 minutes. Allow to cool.

Mix in:
2 pounds ricotta cheese
¾ cup powdered sugar
chocolate, finely grated
toasted almonds, finely chopped

Make sure the pieces of chocolate and nuts are small enough that they won't clog the tip of your pastry bag.

Easy Cannoli Filling

Mix together:
2 pounds ricotta cheese
1 cup powdered sugar
¾ cup chocolate, finely grated
almonds, finely chopped
1½ teaspoons cinnamon
Fold in:
½ pint heavy cream, whipped

Pipe the filling of your choice into the shells using a pastry bag with a decorative tip, if desired. Dust the filled cannoli lightly with powdered sugar. Either recipe makes about two dozen cannoli.

Sunday, November 10

Y ou'd think it would be hard for five adult sisters to get together as often as we do. We range in age from 22 (me) to 41 (Lucy). But we love drama, and this one would fill a void. It had been a while. The last big family drama went on for years and ended only when our brother Frankie finally came home and married his high school sweetheart, breaking the restless family spell. It was actually an ancient spell cast a couple of thousand years before and it came to a head with the Vietnam War. At least that was how Mom and I told it—our imagined sequel to the Tale of the Last Cannoli.

Frankie had been home from Vietnam for a few years but was wandering the country, a lost soul, hanging out in San Francisco with hippies, perhaps other injured and traumatized Nam vets. Maybe they were collectively contemplating the meaning of life, death, war, family. No one knew. When he came home he moved forward and never looked back. Unlike Dad, whose newly surfaced war diary gave clues to his unexplained dark moods.

The startling news I had to share today was that we, Dad's ten children, had not been the first to hear his Tale of the Last Cannoli. My sisters and I had met up and were strolling around Rahway Park. It was crisp and sunny and we could see our breath. It was getting close to Thanksgiving and we talked of food and what our brothers would be cooking up for the crowd. Vinnie and his wife Dana were the main chefs. The other boys would be sous-chefs.

I made the revelation. "You're not going to believe this, but Dad told that tale to one of his war buddies. His name was Buddy Higgins."

"How do you know?"

"Yeah, right. Carmela, you were not even a spark in Dad's eye back in the 1940s."

"Well, not to get too graphic, but I was a spark somewhere else, if not in his eye."

"Between him and Mom—don't forget she had some latent sparks too," said Rena.

"So how do you know this?" Maria asked.

"Dad's war diary."

I turned to look at my four sisters with my tigereyes and sure as sunshine, their eyes turned to sapphire, emerald, topaz, and ruby.

My story, the details I knew, flowed like a Greek myth, a fairy tale, like one of Aesop's fables, moral to be deciphered.

"No, I didn't read it all. Mom has been reading it on the sly. Dad thinks she confiscated it. She felt so bad when she read his writing that he hoped he'd be 'a better father than a soldier.' "

I told them what I had gleaned: that when Dad was in New Guinea, all the soldiers wrote V letters home to their wives and families. "They had to write on manual type-writers. The letters were often censored—you could see blacked out lines. They were also allowed to keep diaries of day-to-day happenings, and most of them did. Seems that Buddy's journal was lost or destroyed in action and Dad's was sent to Buddy's widow by mistake. That would be Mom's friend LouAnn Harris. She put it away until recently when she discovered it belonged to one Vincent Giuseppe Donitella. She tracked down Dad and Mom easy enough—they're the only Donitella in the Rahway phone book. Dad's been in his melancholy mood ever since. The diary probably reminds him of what happened to Buddy.

"Long story short, Buddy was in a deep blue funk because someone wrote him that his wife, LouAnn, was going out on him. Not true at all. But Buddy took it out on a blindfolded Japanese prisoner by shooting him. Dad freaked out and was going to report Buddy to be disciplined. But the Japanese Zeros started strafing and in the confusion, Dad got to safety. They found Buddy's destroyed body next day. Something called a daisy cutter got him."

"Daisy cutter? Sounds like a tool for art," Maria said.

"Or for making cookies," Lucy said.

"Well, he was in ribbons . . . But before that happened Buddy was envious of Dad's getting love letters from Mom. So Dad told Buddy the Tale of the Last Cannoli, just as he would tell it to his kids that he didn't even know yet. It's written down in the yellowing pages of that typed journal.

That was why LouAnn thought it was so important to get Dad's journal back to him. Only it's Mom and I who are savoring his words. LouAnn was overwhelmed by Dad's way with words."

The brilliant gemstone eyes lowered, raised.

"Well, I think it's great," I said firmly. "Dad's story should be preserved as his legacy. Imagine, it goes back to, what, 1941? Like the Last Cannoli."

Silence. Reverential or something else?

I didn't tell them how I had met with Old Carmela and deconstructed Dad's story. I imagined I would deconstruct the story differently every time I thought of it. I told them not to mention the journal for now. "Mom thinks Dad doesn't want his sons to read the journal. But there is nothing in it for him to be ashamed of," I said. "LouAnn thinks he should have gotten the medal. Not Buddy."

"It would take an act of Congress to get it straight," Lucy said.

"I don't think Dad cares," I said.

"We don't care," chimed in Maria and Teresa.

I told them, "I just think it's valuable to think of Dad, a 21-year-old soldier, telling this mushy tale to another soldier. Apparently to dig him out of the blues."

And a tale he had held on to all these years, compressed into one petrified frozen cannoli in all the freezers we've ever had, going on 44 years.

Monday, November 11, Veterans Day

Veterans Day was unseasonably warm this year. With a touch of irony it was still Indian summer. Most leaves had been raked, piled, and burned to ashes. The leaves that remained fluttered brown and lonely. It felt not really sad, but melancholic. Perhaps the uncertainty and doubts I was overloaded with lately were the real cause, not the weather or the long-ago wars that cut down soldiers in their prime, some not even yet in their prime.

My father always marked this holiday with his friends in the Disabled American Veterans or Veterans of Foreign Wars. I still had paper poppies from past events I'd attended with him. He asked me, as a favor, to go with him today to the local Knights of Columbus over on Elizabeth Avenue. He knew I was out of my element now at this age. But I granted his request.

When I arrived my father and a couple of my uncles, also veterans, were gathered around the barbecue grill on the back patio. One of them flipped the burgers and hot dogs. I saw bowls of relish, mustard, ketchup, and mayonnaise.

My father was wearing a T-shirt that flaunted the Italian and American flags and said something about being a proud Italian. Uncle Pete, my mother's brother, was wearing one with an etching of Christopher Columbus on it.

"They want to say he was a bad guy now," Pete said about the recent groundswell of bad press Columbus had gotten. The men all shook their heads and looked more hurt than anything. They had all been initiated into the Knights of Columbus, an honor that had the added bonus of having been extended to them by Irishmen, the previous immigrant community to be vilified in America's pecking order. It would be very hard, and unlikely, for them to let go of Cristoforo Colombo as an Italian American hero. I took some consolation in the irony of them all being sons of recent immigrants who had no bloodline to Columbus, a Genovese or Ligurian of northern Italy who would have looked down on southern Italians. Nor were they related even distantly to the Pilgrims, currently in disfavor as well.

I smiled to myself thinking how at one time, Dad would have gotten on his soapbox about the "denigration" of Italians and gone through a roster of their great contributions to this country—including how Thomas Jefferson wanted Italian, not English, to be our national language. Now he and the other men stood around in baggy pants, T-shirts tucked over bellies, and rubber-soled shoes or sandals. They spoke in their father tongue that mostly eluded me. They referred to their own and others' medical problems nearly sotto voce, because just yesterday that chatter was not manly.

One final puzzle piece returned to my mind. I looked around and saw the tables laden with typical American barbecue food—hot dogs, burgers, sauerkraut, white rolls, potato salad. Only the sausage and meatballs hinted at our heritage. I recalled how last summer some three or four generations of our family, about 30 or 40 people, got together for a big picnic. It was held at the Gran Centurions in Clark, a private club founded in 1966 "to foster and perpetuate the rich heritage of Italian ancestry, culture and history." I remembered the women sitting around calmly chatting, like the men at this afternoon's gathering. I couldn't tell how many were bored, biding time and wishing they were elsewhere. But they'd come because *la famiglia* was everything, and even I had to admit its centripetal force. I concluded with mixed sadness and surrender, *Old Italians don't die, they become American.*

Later, I finished up helping my father at his produce stand. We closed up the green-and-white awnings, covered some of the produce, put crates in the back. I put the ripest fruits in one of our two walk-in refrigerators. Lately the smaller one had been kept padlocked. Dad stored the cash register, his books, and occasionally a large sum of money there. Only he had the lock's combination. I was glad he didn't ask me to help with his accounts. Numbers made me anxious. Preferring words, ideas, and concepts, I had majored in English and looked forward to teaching it at Mother Seton's all-girls Catholic high come January.

My father helped me load up some of the fruits and

vegetables to share with my sisters. We hugged and kissed good-bye.

Dad always made it feel as if each parting was our last one, he held so tight. "Be good, say your prayers, Godspeed, see you tomorrow." Fletcher and Hampton, Dad's workers at the produce stand, would say, "See you tomorrow, God willing and the creek don't rise." All my aunts, uncles, and grandparents—Grandma Coniglio now the only grandparent left—made parting an extended slow-release ritual.

I started to drive home to Linden the usual way, in case my father noticed. Then I made a U-turn and headed to old Peterstown, also known as the Berg, still inhabited mostly by Italians. I found the address I wanted and pulled over. I had balled up my courage and decided to go talk to Sammy Bono, the wise guy. I actually found him sitting on his stoop.

In my head, to calm my pulse, I was practicing the old cliché, *Sammy, I'm gonna tawk nice first* . . . The silliness of it helped me relax. I breathed deep and strolled up the walk as if he were expecting me.

He recognized me as Vincent's daughter. "Well, *ch' se dic*? Whatta ya say?"

"Excuse me, Mr. Bono. I hope you remember me."

Sammy said, "Yeah, I remember you. Carmela. You're Vincent's baby."

"Yes, I'm the youngest of the ten."

He seemed to relax now too. "That was you, I think, in the shadows at the Villa Roma last week, during my friendly visit. What can I do you for, Baby? Spoiled?"

"No such thing with my parents."

"Ha, you don't know what you're missing."

"Perhaps. I was wondering if we could talk about something . . ."

"Sure, sure, we can talk." He picked up a baseball and started bouncing it back and forth between his two hands. "Neighbor kids must've hit it here."

"Well, you see, I don't think it's a good idea you should store hot watches at our family produce stand. I was wondering if you could find another place to store them?"

"Hot what? Watches?"

He looked genuinely puzzled. I was speechless after that.

"I'm not sure what you're talking about."

"Please, Mr. Bono."

"What's with the mister, call me Sammy."

"I know you have influence in the neighborhood."

"Yeah? Where'd you hear that? Some *mamaluke*?"

You're the mamaluke, I wanted to say, *if you think I'm born yesterday.*

I had to catch my breath. I thought he looked a lot like John Garfield in an old movie I just saw, *Body and Soul.* I had to get past his handsome looks. He had done a rotten thing. Now he was saying, "Maybe one of them *mulingians*, works for your father—they tell you some cock-and-bull story about watches?"

At first I heard "Moe and John" and looked quizzical. Sammy said, "You know, the *tut' sun'.*" Oh, he meant Fletcher and Hampton. I recognized the old Italian nicknames for Blacks—*mullingians*, from *melanzana* or *eggplant*, and *tut' sun'* or "all sound," referring to African

Americans' songs. Neither sounded as degrading as what some whites called Blacks. But still, I knew better. I knew from racial epithets.

I recalled how Dad used to say, "They have to stay on their own side"—until Fletcher tried to buy a modest house in a nice neighborhood of Elizabeth. He had worked hard for years to save the large down payment required. He had decent credit. He even had the plumbing and electrical skills to fix up the place and make a good home for his wife, son, and two daughters.

And not a single bank would grant him a loan.

Dad didn't have to think twice. He cosigned on a home loan for Fletcher, putting up his produce business as collateral.

The business was the only asset my father owned. Now that he needed money to renovate the mansion, he had nothing else to use for collateral.

Fletcher did not know this. And Dad would never tell him.

"If you're referring to Fletcher or Hampton, Mr. Johnson or Mr. James to you, they are not eggplants or *mullingians*. And no, they would not have told me such a thing. *Mamaluke* yourself."

"Hey, hey, don't get testy, young'un."

I stared, boring my gaze hard as diamond through him. He didn't even squirm.

Hoping to get results, I softened my approach. "I'm just asking you to look into it. My father works so hard, *honest* hard. My big brothers and sisters don't like to see someone take advantage of him."

"That s'posed to scare me?

"I didn't mean to. But if it gets you to act."

Sammy gave what seemed to be a nervous giggle. Then out of the blue he went on for a while about his upbringing. He shed a few tears when he mentioned how his grandmother had raised him. Then he quickly wiped the tears and smirked.

"All right, Carmela Baby. Yer scaring me what with that huge clan of yours. Not. I'll see what I can do. But you know, I can't make any promises I can't keep."

"I understand. *Promise* ain't in your vocabulary." He flinched at that.

"Watchit, show respect for your elders."

I stood my ground. "Thank you for hearing me out. I really appreciate it. My brothers will appreciate it too."

I watched a couple of Black teens ride by on bikes. Sammy opened his mouth to say something but then grimaced and tossed his baseball faster. "No problem, Carmela Baby. I'll be in touch."

I seriously doubted that.

"Don't call me Baby, only my family is allowed to."

He saluted me and stared at the Black boys.

Tuesday, November 12

"We have everything we need here in this old gray city of Elizabeth," Hampton said to me. Like most Blacks in the Northeast, his family had migrated from the South—in his case from a small town outside Boone, North Carolina, in the Blue Ridge Mountains, shortly after he was born. I had come to relieve him and Fletcher until my father arrived. To hear them talk about the old country ways—the food, the old-timers who would never set foot outside their small town where people still left keys in cars, didn't lock front doors—was like hearing my parents talk about Sicily. There might have been a huge spatial distance between the two Old Countries, but there was a similar sense of loss and grief, a sort of burnishing of memory. For me those memories, burnished or not, were soul food.

Fletcher, also from the South, continued, "Right about that, Hamp. Nocera's, Bella Palermo, the Saturday market, and best of all Donitella's Produce."

"Don't forget the corner fields that grow greens only old

Italians know how to pick," I chimed in. I appreciated how Dad's longtime help, now family friends, paid tribute to the venerable Italian places. They used to be called "the colored boys" from Frog Hollow, the historically African American neighborhood. They had been helping Dad since the late 1950s, when the burgeoning business was no more than a small open-air stand. I knew what they really loved: Over the years I'd heard them discussing how much they loved the fish restaurant on Trumbull Street and the new Portuguese café on Monroe Avenue. They loved that Dad got them collards, not readily available in mainstream supermarkets. Turns out they also loved a pasta with pig's feet—few of us did—that one of the old Italian customers shared with them. Dad loved it too. He seemed to think everything was delicious, after what he had to eat overseas during the war.

Just as we all got Dad to stop saying *Jap*, we got him with the times, referring to his old buddies as *Black* if not *African American,* no longer *colored boys*. "What's in a name," he would crow, "if you love the person?" We explained, he listened. At first he didn't get that *mullingian* and *tut' sun'* were not only unflattering and demeaning, but fed into a greater looming threat to Blacks. In his mind these were terms of affection—until we compared them with *guinea, wop, dago*, and *greaseball,* and then he made the connection. It helped when he remembered an Irish classmate in grammar school singing, "Dago left, dago right, dago wop wop wop." We laughed when Dad told us that singsong ditty and how he had socked the lad in the kisser.

Dad, famous for pontificating on his pet issues, for saying, "Everyone is entitled to my opinion," was also famous for giving people nicknames to match their characters. He started to call me Cat Girl, because he said he never heard me enter the room. I was trying to be a fly on the wall and just listen to everyone else who was older, more worldly, more experienced.

I hadn't seen Fletcher or Hampton in a long time. These days they only helped Dad when I was not available. They were getting on in years, like Dad, feeling this or that joint, going gray at the temples. Seeing me must've sparked an old memory for Hampton, one of the many that I had only heard about secondhand.

"How goes your brother Vinnie, one who used to work here back in high school?" he said.

"He goes fine, happily married to Dana, the girl next door, dancing, both of them cooking with fire."

"Never forget the day someone at home—believe it was you—got seriously hurt. Your dad and Vinnie came to work with a look on their faces we will never forget till our dying day. Ain't it so, Fletch?"

I knew what day Hampton meant, so before he could continue I said, "I bet that was the day my father couldn't finish one of his famous family stories, so Vinnie took over and did it for him. Vinnie told me about it."

Hampton looked puzzled. But I didn't want to be reminded of those long-ago burns that I could not remember. I continued hastily. "Vinnie says my father was driving around in circles that day and trying to tell a story about Sicily, but he couldn't keep his mind on it. It was the one about how his father came to leave that beautiful isle. He couldn't stop driving in circles, and he couldn't finish the story. So Vinnie—he was only 13 then—said, 'Dad, I'll take over.' *Grandpa . . . he came from Sicily, the crossroads of the world, where life was always a mixed blessing, like the fico d'India, the prickly pear. The juice ran sweet but it sent stickers under the skin and gave a mouthful of seeds. One old villager loved his land so much that every day he grabbed two fistfuls of it with horse manure mixed in and said he wanted to be eaten by the worms of Sicily so the sun could turn him into the food his people eat.*

"Vinnie finished the story for Dad, and it worked. Dad was late but he parked the car."

"Hmmm, yes." Hampton scratched his head. "Your father speechless was, is, a rare occasion. I remember now . . . was hot water . . ."

I interrupted. "Why don't you both fill up bags with the new mess of greens Dad just brought in. They're lush."

"Sure thing. This the only place sells the variety we like."

After they left, I sprayed the lettuces. I noticed how iceberg, still the darling of many, was now going the way of Wonder bread as people discovered the dark greens— lamb's-quarters, mesclun, arugula, each a version of bitter, peppery, grassy, earthy, herby. Not just water and crunch, like that wetlands of islands for an earthworm that iceberg was.

Ripe fruit from southern Jersey. The Garden State was not exactly Sicily's Garden of Eden, but it was close enough, especially in summer and fall, for the Italian immigrants who had poured into Ellis Island in the early 1900s. Fruit and vegetable surplus went to the Salvation Army on East Jersey Street.

I sat on a sturdy crate and cleared my head of others' memories. I read the *Star-Ledger*—nothing of interest. I scanned the produce tables again for trapdoors. Silly thing to do.

My father and Old Carmela arrived about the same time conversing excitedly in Sicilian, neither coming up for air. Her eyes bored like gold nuggets into my eyes. She didn't mention my visit. She asked for a *cucuzza*. Dad gave her one long crooked one and quoted that old proverb in Sicilian, "Two things the Lord can't straighten out, *cucuzza* and hard heads." They laughed carefree and easy.

Even with their rapid Sicilian I understood the gist of what they said. I could not speak a full sentence of the dialect. Only words, mostly imperatives, *mangia, sta' zit, ven aca, ma fangool, fa Napoli*. Or was it *va Napoli*? In the radiant light that emanated from Old Carmela, I briefly understood time. Deep time, stretching back to the ancestral land that was once fertile, that once fed the Romans, that was Greek, Phoenician, Elymian, filled with goddess worship—the Sicily I learned about beyond what my father told us. Through space and time, the sailing of the Palatine ships from Hamburg to the dingy gray streets of Elizabeth. The golden nugget gleam of her eyes played out the mystery in ways I knew I would only come to understand with age.

They were reminiscing about Old Carmela's home in Agrigento, the same province my four grandparents came from. She told stories I'd heard before about how life was hard but very beautiful in her village, Mussomeli. Then, as if contradicting her own statement, she spoke a phrase I'd heard many times from old Sicilians: *"Ma cu' cunta ci menti 'a iunta."* It meant something like every time you tell a story you lie or add a little to it. But she added another phrase I knew, *"Ma quannu si cunta e nenti,"* who speaks her troubles sets herself free. When she switched to Dad's stories, she spoke as if quoting the Bible or Greek mythology or both.

"Even the rocks, even the wind sang!" Old Carmela knew that story of Dad's and sang its most famous line to him. *"Come stai, figlio mio?"*

"Tutt' é bene, Signora. No c'é senso lamentarmi." My father sang his lines too. He faced east and south and stared off in the direction of Sicily. He chanted in Sicilian, "Seasons turn. A seed is planted. A plant is seeded. Another child appears at my table. Another mouth to feed. All I really wanted was not to be piss poor but to be a priest. My father had to stop me. He said I could never be still enough for the contemplative life."

He and Old Carmela both smiled weakly as he said all this as if it was such old material, lines being fed to him by some invisible prompter.

Then he gave his spiel about Sicily, the Garden of Eden, the one Vinnie once had to finish for him. "Ah, but Sicilia! Sicily was the most spectacular place on earth. Its coast was blessed with warm sandy beaches and rocky bluffs. Tongues of sapphire water lapped at the sweet, pure land and the sun poured warm gold over the rugged red cliffs. For Sicily was the most wild and free, with a spirit so full of music and rhythm . . ."

Old Carmela repeated, "*Si*, Vinnie, I remember, *dimmi, anche le rocce, anche il vento cantava.*" Even the rocks, even the wind sang.

I felt her ancient glittering eyes were telling me there was nothing new to discover or learn. I knew it all. Maybe Madeleine was trying to tell me the same. I wasn't sure. Lately there was more urgency in Madeleine's apparitions. I would try to listen more closely next time she came to me in a dream.

As my father and Old Carmela conversed about nothing and everything, from the weather to someone's child's missteps, I thought of what my mother had told my sisters and me. "Your father was good with words. Grandma wanted me to marry someone more . . . sophisticated and well-to-do. But what your father lacked in riches, he made up for in words, stories, songs. He had a lot of feeling. At least before the war."

"But the war was over so long ago," we said. "Before we were even born."

"Not for your father. Remember what he said about the big things?"

I glanced up at the prominently placed sign reading DONITELLA'S PRODUCE MARKET. Dad was so proud of it, one dream that had come to pass. He loved the fruits of the earth and he had the pleasure of handling and selling them.

Fletcher and Hampton were assisting me with fruit and

vegetable arrangements. Infected with Dad's pride, I swept my arm over the colorful exotics, pointing and naming each.

"We've started carrying all these imports thanks to Elizabeth's Latino immigrants," I bragged. "Breadfruit, carambola, cherimoya, feijoa, guava, kumquat, passion fruit, pepino . . . If it were up to Dad, he'd carry only the standard Italian greens."

Hampton said, "That's what's known as peaceful co-existence—Ital, American, Latino, and what all side by side."

We laughed and I picked up a hose to spray the lettuce. "Speaking of which, I guess you'll meet our native African nun, Sister Julieta, soon."

"Saturday night," said Fletcher. "We volunteered to bring our American-style mess of greens."

"I bet she'll love it. Dad says she's very down-to-earth for a nun."

I saw Dad finish up serving a customer and approach us. Indulging in routine banter with the men, he said, "Everything copacetic, Fletch, Hamp?"

Hampton jumped on the banter. "You bet, Vinnie, too early—or too late?—to be dis-co-nun-gi-ated."

Dad swept his arm in an arc as if to clear a stage and showed off his shim-sham tap step. The two men clapped. Then he stopped to help Fletcher and Hampton unload crates. They placed the fruit and vegetables on tables with signs giving prices and names. All the while they continued to kibitz playfully. I kept spraying greens and watching pensively until Dad said, "I'll relieve you, Cat."

I handed Hampton the hose, grabbed my briefcase from a chair, and readied to depart. "Enjoy Sister Julieta," I said to Hampton and Fletcher.

Dad followed me to my car and put a bag of produce in my trunk.

Suddenly he was very stern. "Before you leave, a word of warning. Do not mingle in my business. If I need help I have four sons."

I swallowed. "Um . . . not sure what business . . ."

"I have spoken," he said.

A baby blue voice came out of my mouth anyway. "You're talking . . . about . . ."

Wednesday, November 13

We had hugged, we had cried together. We laughed, ate, and prayed together. We feasted, occasionally fasted, together. We mourned and memorialized our dead together.

But we never talked about wounds. Reading my father's war diary, I realized this and a few other things. My father had been hit by some shrapnel but, in his own words, "begged my CO not to send me home." The company officer was only too glad to keep Dad in that jungle. Later Dad regretted that decision.

Driving to my brother Frank's restaurant in Asbury Park, I contemplated these things. Things I knew nothing about firsthand. I once asked Maria and Teresa why no one else in the family ever mentioned my burns if they were so bad. They shrugged, then said something I hadn't considered. Teresa said, "Maybe because it hurt us more than it hurt you, I guess. We all suffered through your injury and the uncertainty of your rehab." It occurred to me then that my lack of light, of consciousness, which I had yet to develop at two years old, was the source of their pain. You would think I'd have some buried pain of trauma. But I think that my mother and father's loving care during that period somehow diminished any lasting effects. Deep focused attention has its own healing power.

I was bringing Frankie crates of Italian winter greens from Dad. These were just starting to show up, along with other so-called exotic produce, in American supermarkets—Swiss chard, broccoli rabe, dandelions, escarole or chicory, and of course Frank's signature *god-dunes*. The best were still served only in Italian trattorias like Frank's Casa Magdalena.

At the top of his menus was printed THE WORLD WILL END WHEN THERE ARE NO MORE DOG-GONE GOD-DUNES, with a little line drawing of the wild thistle. He served the *god-dunes* three ways, breaded and fried in olive oil, marinated and braised in marsala stock, and fried in olive oil and garlic topped with a grating of ricotta salata.

Frank never talked about Nam. It was patently understood not to ask. It was more than a dozen years ago that he finally returned home and married Charlene.

After we unloaded the produce we sat and chatted. He made us some strong espresso, which always unlocks tongues the way Gramps's wine does. I ventured slowly into deep waters. I felt I could with Frankie. I asked if he knew that Mom's new friend LouAnn had just discovered she had Dad's war diary all these years.

He looked up briefly from his paperwork and said nonchalantly, "Hmmm, think I heard something about that."

He was inputting numbers in his calculator so I waited a bit.

"Not interested in reading it?"

"Nah." He totaled whatever he was calculating and put his papers aside.

"There are interesting tidbits—like how the soldiers made moonshine out of potato peels and other . . . vegetable matter."

"That right?"

"The day Dad came back from the war he was a different man, Mom said."

"Yep."

"It's not just soldiers who carry the weight of war. It touches everyone in the family."

"Yep."

"Being a wounded Vietnam vet can you attest to that?" He banged his demitasse cup down. It seemed unintentional.

"Nam's not in the torrid zone like New Guinea. You like the espresso? It's a special brand of beans I order from Frisco—Graffeo, it's called."

"I thought you used Torrefazione."

"I alternate, sometimes mix."

"I'll have another, *per favore*." As he was grinding the beans and making the espresso, I went into my spiel—you'd have thought I was the war wounded. Before sitting down he put some tunes on the jukebox. The first was "Danny Boy," a song about a young soldier. Our father loved it, even though it was Irish.

"You know how Dad wants to adopt ten more kids, one for each of us, ha! Got me wondering why. Then this journal shows up out of nowhere and I wonder if siring, adopting all these kids is a way of compensating for some of the war dead. Not that he writes about doing any of the killing himself. He was mostly repairing aircraft." I thought I saw Frank grimace at *killing*.

I went on, "Dad wasn't the only one affected by his war experience. Mom had to bear the burden of worrying about him every day. And she had to take care of Mario, too. The whole family, innocents, are impacted. It's a ripple effect, even into the distant future. And it's something that stays with you long after the war is over." Not sure how I would have known that but I may have picked it up from recent antinuke literature.

I took a few breaths and said, "That's why it's so important to remember the sacrifices made not just by the soldiers, but by their families as well. We must learn from the past and strive for peace in the future."

The next song on the jukebox was Frank Sinatra's "Young at Heart." The hiss of the espresso machine was covering my rambling but I thought I heard Frank utter, "Amen" as he set down my steaming cup. "You know how to *espress* yourself."

"*Si,*" I sighed, feeling hypercaffeinated. I added two lumps of sugar and stirred. A plate of *biscot'* appeared.

"Better watch out, remember how Dad used to tell us if you drank too much coffee . . ."

"You'd disappear," I finished with him and we laughed recalling the stories Dad used to tell. Always Dad stories— the best distraction in a family of ten where none got to be number one for very long.

One of Dad's stories was about his mythical brother Joe who disappeared from drinking too much coffee. We believed him because coffee made us jittery and we were sure that would make us disappear after a while.

"I thought it was the Popsicle sticks and the end of world?"

"It came to me as *god-dunes* when I was in Frisco."

"Guess you had some fun out west there."

"It was a time of limbo, but yeah, some memorable moments."

I found Frank was willing to talk about the time after he came home from the war and had wandered away from family and friends to San Francisco. He got up and made himself another espresso—no sugar, just lemon peel. "Learned that in Frisco too in the Italian neighborhood."

"What was it like?"

"Okay, since we are both veterans of Dad's war, I'll share a bit with you. You're sworn to secrecy. Don't want Charlene to ever know."

I was more than used to how we all had secrets and pretended to share them with one person and no one else. My baby-of-the-family status was earning me trust.

"Cross my heart, may Grandpa Donitella's spirit strike me deaf, dumb, and blind."

Frankie

I hooked up with a commune of hippies. There was a woman, Saffron she called herself. We picked each other up on a grassy hill in Golden Gate Park where all the dudes were smoking, playing bongos, and Saffron was twirling like a living bolt of gauze. I stayed with her a while in a crash pad on Ashbury. Despite my resistance she got it in her head I should meet her roshi from Japan and sit meditation with him. He had come all the way from Japan to open the first Zen Buddhist temple in the U.S.

"What a schmuck," I told her. "I heard about these gurus—drive around in Rolls-Royces."

"What did you say, Frankie?"

"Nothing. I said I wish him luck."

"No you didn't, honey."

"I said it in Yiddish."

"Roshi can handle you. When you were in Thailand and Japan, did you ever hear chanting?"

"I heard the hum of birds, insects, choppers, and at times I'd hear my father's words." Yeah, I was scared. You never know in combat, in the heat of battle, you never know what you're doing. You are untouchable in combat. If you start thinkin' you get the runs. Death can't happen to you.

"No, I don't know what a chant sounds like," I told Saffron. Her roshi laughed a lot, a high pitch. Saffron sat like him, legs tied in a pretzel. They were kind enough to supply me a chair due to my injured leg. I asked the roach, I mean Rosh, "Where does Buddhist grace come from?"

"Come from same place as all grace," he said.

"Where is that, sir?"

"The three treasures."

"Okay, Roach," I said, "enough with the lists already. Saffron had told me about the others, what were they? Four *kinds of truth, eight ways to walk down your path, three of this, six of that . . . What else Confucius say?"*

"That's Taoism, Frankie," Saffron said, "not Buddhism."

Roach chimed in, "Not Taoism, not Buddhism." Tinkling laugher. His bald head stayed still and his grin stretched from ear to ear. The guy was pretty congenial, I gotta admit. Not at all like what I was taught to expect from a monk. But when he stared through those familiar slanted eyes and said nothing he made me nervous. I chattered, "At least you keep things tidy with lists. Not like the Catholics who keep adding and subtracting mysteries, depending on advances in science." What I really liked about that Roshi-rama—I laughed with him, pretty hard. It was the first time in three months I heard my own laugh. Saffron and I got up to leave. I said, "Roshi, sayonara. It's great, both of us find a handle in the grace."

Saffron and I headed back to her pad. I told her, "That Jap is the first holy one I've ever met."

"Japanese, please," Saffron says. "How would you like to be called a wop?"

"Depends on who's doing the calling. I didn't mean no harm to the guy, but it's Japs when my father's fighting World War II."

"It's 1970. Doesn't he know the war has been over for 25 years?"

She had a point.

Back at her pad the kids were serving bean turd, tofu this or that. I craved food with bones, crunch, chutzpah. So we walked around looking for something familiar. At one small market I asked the clerk if they had finocchio to nosh on.

He gave me a dark stare and said, "Go to North Beach for that sort of perverted stuff." Saffron explained that Finocchio's was the name of a place, a show with a gay she-who-is-a-he, whatta you call them . . . I said, "Let's look for god-dunes as we walk by fields. The world will end when there are no more." We never found them but we came across some eggplants in a shop. I showed Saffron how to tell a male from a female eggplant and we bought a male.

We ended up at a Black church, I think it was in the Fillmore district. Met a Floyd and Betty there during their rousing service. I remember now. The singing was loud and mighty. Church was so full we had to sit in the choir loft. I held my eggplant in my left hand and swayed with it. My right hand rose up to my heart. The eggplant fell and rolled out of my reach. The minister spread his arms and threw back his head like he was ready to fly into the choir. Everyone started clapping to:

The river is deep and the river is wide
Hallelujah
Milk and honey on the other side . . .

"Sing it, brother!" said Betty, the woman next to me. When the singing was over, I heard the man behind me say to his neighbor, "If there's a heaven, Floyd, they're paying to get us in!"

"I hear ya! But don't mind waiting to find out, no sir!" said Floyd with a deep grainy voice that made me homesick. They invited me and Saffron for supper later in the *audiorium. Wouldn't you know it—someone had found and cooked the eggplant, breaded and fried. Still recall that meal after all these years, drumsticks and wings, sweet yam pie, a mess of collard greens smoky with pork butt, meltaway biscuits, and cornbread. The turkey gravy had so much body, it seemed to have a soul. Come to think of it, it was Thanksgiving. Suddenly I was homesick for our Thanksgiving back home on Creek Street and I remember saying to Saffron when we got back to her flat I was going to call Mom. I was almost ready to come home.*

I remember the one little thing that got me wanting to see Mom. Saffron's eyes must have filled with tears after I said something crude to her, can't recall what, probably was my displaced anger about war. Her eyes turned red. I thought, That's not at all like Mom who knows from barbs and grenades without ever having set foot in a war zone. Who walked the combat zone of our father's mind field like she was asbestos. Our mother had no false pity, no false piety. Luxuries she couldn't afford, between our father and the ten of us.

As Frankie finished his story I was beginning to perceive the wounds we didn't talk about not as the elephant in the room, but as the gazelle loping from the distant past, jockeying to land with a thud in the present.

Friday, November 15

I stopped by Mom and Dad's early. It had rained good and hard and I wanted to check the creek in our backyard where we used to play, heedless of the slick surface rainbow washing by from the plastic and chemical factories in Linden, the next town over. Now the creek flowed ruddy amber, the color of the clay banks. The nearby garden that produced lush food was like the boy in the bubble who died last year, protected by an invisible membrane from poisons and pathogens. It wasn't those toxins that had caused Madeleine's death.

Inside the house I sat in Mom's rocking chair. Mom was in her room. Dad was sleeping in for a while. His loyal workers, Fletcher and Hampton, were taking care of setting up the produce stand that would be crawling with customers by 9 a.m. I started going through a small stack of newspapers. The house filled with the tantalizing aromas of percolating coffee and reheated pizza. To my surprise Mario came through the front door.

"What are you doing here so early?" I asked.

"I saw your car out front."

"That old heap—usually people hear it before they see it." A push-button automatic Chrysler, the last of 1965. He looked at my heap of papers.

"Catching up on current events? You know they never change."

"I suppose. Some eccentric News Central just rotates them every generation or so."

"Right—war, murder, political corruption, Hollywood scandal, war, murder, political corruption . . . repeat."

"Ad nauseam."

"Well, anyway you can impress the impressionable at the next cocktail party."

"If I ever get invited to one." Mario was on his way to Rutgers—he taught advanced physics at either Newark or New Brunswick depending on the day. His classes always had a long waiting list of students, probably because he made physics, even for the brainiacs, sound like a fairy tale. The storytelling urge just ran in the family.

"Anyway, what brings you here?" I asked.

"Told Mom I'd stop by for coffee and a chat. Tell her how her grandkids are doing."

How times had changed. Used to be her daughters who coffee-chatted with Mom. I quickly folded the Newark *Star-Ledger* and laid it on top of the *Elizabeth Daily Journal, New York Times,* and *Washington Post.* Didn't want my brother to know just how current I was keeping. I was looking for reports of theft, specifically stolen watches, constantly expanding my radius. I had recently stopped by the Elizabeth police station near Dad's business but got no relevant information about theft, watches or other. The closest I'd come to finding any news like that was in the *New York Times* police blotter a week or so ago:

At approximately 9:00 p.m., the New York City Police Department received a report of a robbery at a high-end jewelry store on the Upper East Side of Manhattan. According to eyewitnesses, a group of armed men entered the store and began to smash display cases and grab jewelry and other valuables. Suspects were reported to be wearing dark clothing and woolen ski masks, making it difficult to identify them. Witnesses also reported hearing gunfire, and at least one person was seen leaving the scene in a black windowless van. Police found the store in disarray, with shattered glass and jewelry strewn across the floor. NYPD has launched an extensive investigation into the robbery, with detectives currently combing through surveillance footage and interviewing witnesses in the area.

Farther on, a news item noted, "This marks one of the most audacious robberies to occur on the Upper East Side in recent history." Except, the item reported, no jewels were taken.

After the mess was cleaned up, a careful inventory showed that nothing was missing. The police are considering the possibility of a decoy burglary as there were reports of several simultaneous heists at Upper East Side residences, including one owned by socialite philanthropist Mrs. Aurora A. Addis. Jewels, heirlooms, and other valuables were taken, possibly by one of the infamous cat burglars.

Sheesh, there's more than one?

"Hey Mario, what are the most expensive watches available?" My brother had good taste, good as in classy and expensive.

"Is this a trick question?"

"No, no . . . I was just curious, no special reason . . . ya' know, maybe someday we can all chip in and buy Mom and Dad nice timepieces."

"Time, time, time . . . can't live with it, can't live without it. But must live within it."

"Is that physicist's talk—Mario's Theory of the Time Paradox?"

"I might use that."

"Be my guest."

"Want to hear more about the space-time continuum?"

"Save it for Carmine."

"Did you know that there is a Latin American country where the clock hands move counterclockwise?"

"Get out."

"They believe the past is in front of us, the future behind."

"Next you'll be telling me the old cliché that time is a way of keeping everything from happening at once," I said smugly.

"Oh no. Some Eastern religions believe that everything is happening at once."

"That's scary." I thought that if so, we already knew how Sonny Bono and the watch fiasco would end. "All right, back to watches—isn't Rolex the most expensive high-end?" I had been able to get a glimpse of Sammy's watch at the Villa Roma before Big Frank stowed it.

"Holy cow, no. It boasts precision, durability, and iconic design. But it's just the one with the broadest renown among the, let's say, nouveaux riches, of which by definition, I am one."

"You mean . . . no don't tell me . . . you've given up your lower-middle-class, or is it social-ladder-climbing immigrant family, status?"

Mario laughed. "Call it rising above, the pulling-up-by-bootstrap syndrome."

"Well I guess that makes you true red-white-and-blue, more American than Sicilian now."

"No way! I'm still straddling both sides of the pond. Okay, let's see. Timepieces." As he spieled off a laundry list of names I didn't know, I heard his piano keys keeping another sort of time. "Patek Philippe, known for intricate mechanical movements and timeless—pun intended—designs. Audemars Piguet, luxury sports watches, as in their Royal Oak and Millenary collections. There is Vacheron Constantin, with its long history of handcrafted watchmaking, since about the 1700s. Jaeger-LeCoultre, precision, Reverso and Master Control collections. A. Lange & Söhne—talk about precious metals and intricate detailing! All known for craftsmanship, quality materials, and classic designs. Watches are not only functional but also pieces of art. Limited production increases their exclusivity and value."

"Wow, your knowledge of watches is surpassed only by your skill with the slide rule." I knew there were now more sophisticated instruments for physicists. But once upon a time, Mario had taught me to do simple arithmetic on his slide rule. "Which one are you wearing?"

He pulled up the cuff on his left arm and I admired an oblong crystal over elegant Roman numerals, no second hand, just two antique-shaped black hands, small and big. He told me to look closely to see what might be amiss. I couldn't see it till he pointed out that the Roman numeral for four was written as IIII instead of IV, unheard of. He explained   it was all about looks. The longer numeral balanced the watch face better.

"It goes back to Roman times—hey, they invented Roman numerals so they could change their symbols as they liked."

"Guess my Cinderella watch doesn't make the cut."

"Not yet, or as the fashionable French say, *pas encore.*"

"Zut alors. Anyway, Cinderella is still a fashion statement in my social context—even though the watch hasn't worked for years, since I swam in the neighbors' pool with it."

"Hey, I just remembered, Carmela, I think it was you I saw the other day in Elizabeth on Magnolia Avenue talking to Sammy Bono."

"You think so?" I said.

"I know so. In fact you were taking leave of Sammy."

"What were *you* doing on Magnolia Avenue?"

"I was coming from Dad's produce stand. And don't change the subject."

"Which is?"

"You don't want to be cavorting with that hood."

"Hmmm, you're right . . . um . . . I wasn't *cavorting*."

"What business could you possibly have with him."

"Okay, if you really want to know, I'll spill. Drop the dime as they say."

"I'm all ears."

"Well, ya' see, it's like this . . . Dad and I stopped by the Villa Roma recently to say hello to Frank, Dad's goombah. And Sammy came in for a quick drink and more or less insulted Dad."

"And? So you decided to go read him the riot act? In person?"

"Let's just say I leaned on him a bit. Now, I'm telling you this, from my lips to your ears . . . Let's just say . . . oh yeah . . . I told Sammy my father had four big strapping sons. And they would not like it if I told them how he insulted Dad."

"What was the insult that was so bad you had to go see him in person?"

"I don't want to repeat it exactly . . ." I was thinking fast. "It was crass, something about Dad's having ten kids—and doing *it* only ten times . . ." That was an easy one to pull out of the bag because we kids often joked about it anyway.

"What a lowlife. Didn't Dad jump on him? That's not something he'd taking sitting down."

"Well, he was about to but Big Frank talked him down,

held him back and kicked Sammy out. Verbally." End of story. I justified my tall tale to myself. I wasn't going to get my brothers involved in this hot goods fiasco. I was pretty sure I, or my sisters and I, could handle this if need be with less drama. Time would tell. Later I would admit to myself that my brothers would never ever share in my devious plan to hijack the hot goods and sell them to get money for Dad's old house and the next ten kids.

Mario seemed to swallow my tale hook, line, and sinker. It could have happened that way. He looked thoughtful. My brothers were all perhaps overly disciplined by our strict father who believed in corporal punishment. So I was not surprised to detect a strong current of compassion in his remarks about Sam.

Mario went on to tell me what he knew about Sammy "the Bull" Bono. He had grown up on the gritty side of Elizabeth, near the Port and the Mariners Mansion, where poverty and violence were a daily reality. His father was a small-time criminal who was frequently in and out of prison, and his mother worked long hours at the Nabisco factory to make ends meet. Sammy had a tough childhood, and had to fend for himself from a young age.

"Sammy quickly learned how to manipulate those around him to get what he wanted," said Mario. "Surprisingly, he excelled in school; he had a sharp mind and a natural talent for numbers. As a teen he was known for his brute strength and ability to think on his feet. He had a straight job for a few years, stocking shelves in the supermarket, but eventually he turned to crime as a way to survive. I think he began by running errands for local mobsters and rose through the ranks, becoming a respected gang member."

Respected sounded overstated but I was enraptured by this complex character study of Sammy the Bull, *Il Toro*. He was often described as charismatic and charming, but with a dark side driven by a need for power and control. I had seen that firsthand.

"Despite his success as a hood," Mario went on, "my guess is that Sammy still struggles with inner demons and feelings of inadequacy stemming from his past. He craves respect and validation. He may have a vulnerable side, but he is cunning and ruthless and will stop at nothing, and you should steer clear of him. Okay? *Gabeesh?*"

"*Si.*"

It crossed my mind that maybe some psychotherapy with my sister Lucy would help the Bull. Fat chance. "Okay, bro," I said firmly, doing the quick palm slap. I meant to keep to that.

I had noticed that despite his rough exterior, Sammy had a code of honor, and he seemed fiercely loyal to his friends and extended family. He had even told me, "I have a soft spot for you, Carmela, I've seen you since you were a pip-squeak."

I didn't tell Mario how Sammy had shed a few tears when he recalled to me how his Sicilian grandmother died when he was still a teen. "She was the only adult who treated me with truly deep love and affection. She spoiled me like no woman has since."

And then my brother Mario answered a question I had

about something my father said back in the Villa Roma that afternoon.

"Keep this under your hat or babushka, I can't tell you all the details . . ."

"Or ya'd hafta kill me."

"Ralph Giordano used to own the plot Dad's produce business is on in Elizabeth."

"*Used* to own?"

"Yeah. For some reason, let's say I don't know, Ralph owed Bono a lot of money and he couldn't pay it fast enough. So he signed the deed over to Bono."

Ah, that explained my father's comment, "He's my landlord. He's got me over a barrel." Dad was not being metaphorical.

"Ralph's in prison for a while," I said.

"He's safer in the hands of the law."

"What a backass piece of luck."

Mom came in the parlor and said, "Mario, come sit with your favorite mother and tell me about my two grandkids."

As they moved into the kitchen, I folded the papers neatly, leaving them all for Dad who would be up soon.

So that's what Sammy Bono was talking about. He now owned the land my father's business was on. Why Ralph Giordano owed Bono a lot of money I couldn't imagine, but he couldn't pay it back on schedule, so he signed the deed over to Sammy. It amazed me to think of Ralph Giordano as lucky to be in prison. "Safer in the hands of the law" sounded like an oxymoron.

Saturday, November 16

My parents had invited a missionary nun to sup with them and wanted me to meet her. I knew Sister Julieta Ntheny was a colleague of one of Dad's relatives in Sicily, Sister Assumption—they had met at a slum orphanage in Nairobi. I didn't know that I would encounter the most beautiful face, skin so smooth and ebony. *Beatific* hardly came close. Certainly we had African American friends, all of them many shades lighter. I was reminded how American Blacks were, voluntarily and involuntarily, diluted by white blood and gene pool, a blending that should have made for a better world. In some ways it had.

But I was bedazzled by the skin, the contrasting white teeth, the quarter-size eyes, a smile so unprepossessing, so disarming. I was speechless.

"*Habari yako!*" she said. "How are you, Carmela?"

"Very fine, and you?"

"Also, *msuri asante*, thanks."

I loved the soft engaging quality of Swahili, even if I didn't know what it meant. It had a resounding classical quality like the Sicilian dialect that Dante so loved.

My next words came out as a non sequitur. "My father says we have a lot of African blood."

Sister Julieta took it in stride and laughed. Her voice was silver wind chimes. She said in an unexpectedly British accent, "Of course. We are all related, one way or another, if one goes back far enough."

"Oh, we don't even have to go back that far . . ." I stopped and realized that I didn't need to say more. She didn't need me to make her feel comfortable with someone who looked white, was mostly white.

I asked how she came to know the daughter of Dad's cousin in Sicily.

"Sister Assumption came for a few months and worked with our orphaned children, helping them learn to read and write. She learned enough English and Swahili. Quite astute for a *mzungu*." Tinkling laughter.

"A what?"

"*Mzungu* is what we Kenyans call white people—you know, the way white Americans have nicknames for Blacks."

Not the same, I thought, but decided not to broach the difference. And Sister Assumption a *mzungu*?

"Your father's cousin learned I was coming to New York to attend a session at the United Nations on the AIDS epidemic, so devastating in my country and much of Africa. Your parents have been so generous and hospitable." AIDS was decimating African families, leaving thousands of children orphaned. Up to that moment it had been almost unreal news, incalculable numbers. Now I was facing someone who had watched her countrymen die before her eyes.

"How was the train from Penn Station?"

"Delightful, so close to your town, to Rahway, yet so far away in character."

"Yes, it's a fast train ride, but it feels like you've traveled at warp speed, gone through a wormhole, and come out in a different universe. I love it."

"Wormhole, indeed!"

I led Julieta upstairs to the small dormer where Lucy, Rena, and Madeleine had slept in the same bed as kids.

"What a cozy little room!"

"That's one way to put it. Slightly bigger than a phone booth." The ceiling slanted toward a window in a narrowed section, barely wide enough to spread your arms. The old double bed had given way to single bunk beds. Sister put her suitcase on top and said she'd sleep on the bottom. On the top one you couldn't sit up without hitting your head on the ceiling.

"Sorry it's so small," I said.

"Oh, *hakuna matata*! It's quite deluxe to my eyes."

She noticed the photos of Lucy, Rena, and Madeleine on the dresser. I told her who each was.

She pointed to Madeleine. It was a goofy photo really, taken in her freshman year, with the Toni perm that Mom used to give all of us girls so she wouldn't have to set our straight hair in curlers each night. Hard to believe, but straight hair was almost obscene then. It was as if displaying that dorky image of Madeleine would make us all miss her less.

"She's the one with the angels now?"

I wanted to joke *Or with the others*, but thought better of it. "Yes, we hope so."

As if Julieta read my expression she said, "Oh you needn't worry. She looks like someone who was always in the state of grace."

"So I've heard," I said, thinking of Rena's story about how Madeleine was a consummate virgin among the eagerly deflowered. "Since I was only seven when she joined the angel brigade."

That brought another tinkling chuckle from Sister. "You're cheeky, eh?"

"Well, can't I be about my own sister?" I was careful not to broadcast my lapsed Catholicism but I found the cheery nun charismatic and easy to chat with. Each of us was saying things that betrayed the subtext of our beliefs— Sister's belief in God, mine in agnosticism.

"Yes, Carmela, you may be cheeky." I loved her Queen's English accent. "It's so good to meet you! How have you been?"

"I've been good, Sister." According to my own bible of sorts, I did not add. I was wondering how things really were in Africa, specifically in Nairobi where Sister worked. I knew that the famines in Ethiopia and the Sudan were dire. And because nonsectarian compassion was on the rise worldwide, people of all religions, or no religion, had come together this past July 13 through the globally televised Live Aid concerts.

"Sister Julieta, are you seeing any of the money raised by Live Aid?"

"Oh, bless me, dear, we hope to. But you know the famine in the Sudan is where they need help yesterday. So we'll see."

Live Aid was the brainchild of Irish rock'n'roller Bob Geldof, who was disgusted by the starvation he had witnessed in Africa in a world of surplus, not to mention waste. He had organized concerts taking place simultaneously in London's Wembley Stadium and JFK Stadium in Philadelphia—16 hours of live music, rock'n'roll on steroids. The event was broadcast around the globe by satellite. Back in 1969 I had not been old enough to be aware when astronauts landed on the moon. But I felt the Live Aid effort was even better and bigger and more world-changing—one rocking big step by man, one giant leap for humankind. I felt connected in peace to every single one of the more than a billion viewers in 110 nations. "It was a triumph of humanitarianism and good will," the *Star-Ledger* wrote. So far more than $125 million had been raised in famine relief for Ethiopia and the Sudan. And it happened because a few generations before me started speaking a lingua franca called rock'n'roll. Now the rest of the world spoke it too.

"I hope you get some help. What are your most pressing needs?"

"School supplies, books, writing materials, desks—as always we need whatever we can get for a good childhood education. And always, clean water."

"How about a CD player? Everyone needs music to nourish the soul." I was thinking but didn't say how music was more important than prayer.

"Right you are. However, we don't always have electricity

in the classrooms. We sing. We use our voices to make music."

"Well, I can support that practice. We can get you a battery-operated one." I recalled one hot summer day when I was young and our electricity was turned off because Mom and Dad had not been able to pay the bill on time. Dad made us sing our family song—more to keep his spirits up than for us.

"By the way," said Julieta with a little fire in her dark eyes. "Freddie Mercury and Queen stole the show, don't you think?"

That floored me. That's when I noticed that Julieta was about my age. Of course she would at least be familiar with contemporary rock. "Yes, my friends are still talking about it. Their 20-minute performance! Unforgettable. Which song did you like best?"

"Of course, 'Bohemian Rhapsody.' Our schoolchildren loved 'We Will Rock You' and 'We Are the Champions.' "

"We *are* the world, Sister Julieta." I wanted to add, *But if there is a Supreme Being why does he/she/it allow such awful suffering as AIDS and famine?* I feared the answer would be *The Lord works in mysterious ways.* Worse, I feared I might swallow that.

Instead I said, "Sister Julieta, you are one cool, cool nun. Wish I'd had one like you in my grammar school."

"I'm sure your Dominican sisters did their best."

"Hmmm, I suppose. Anyway, we survived. We even learned things. But your children, orphans of the AIDS epidemic, how are they faring?"

"It is amazing, as always. Children are so resilient and full of faith. It truly is a humbling experience. The children find ways to be happy and content every day."

Such optimism. But the fact remained that the majority of the world's millions of AIDS cases were in sub-Saharan Africa. I knew that Christian missionaries were preaching abstinence, not safe sex. Maddening. But I couldn't countenance a debate with this lovely sister—if she turned out to agree with that view.

"That sounds wonderful. I'm glad you're able to make such a difference in their lives."

"It doesn't take much to do that. It's all thanks to the grace of God. He guides me every step of the way."

Back to being Jesus's bride. "I can see that you're very dedicated to your work. It must be fulfilling." I was trying to steer the conversation somewhere else . . . away from the God thing.

"It is. And what about you, Carmela? Are you still practicing your faith?"

Nothing like getting right to the point—a bit nervy I thought. "I . . . I haven't been as involved as I used to be. Life gets busy, you know?"

"I understand. But remember, God is always there for you, even in the busiest of times. He just needs you to reach out to him."

"I'll keep that in mind, Sister. Thank you." If I believed, I'd pray for God to support Dad's dream, a win-win. Dad gets his satisfaction and ten of God's lost children get safe harbor.

"*Hakuna matata.* You're most welcome, my dearest."

"What is hockuna myta . . . ?"

"Swahili for no worries—*ha-koo-nah mah-tah-tah.*"

"That'll come in handy."

I asked Sister Julieta if she knew the story about Sister Assumption, the daughter of Dad's cousin. She was one of five girls, four of whom became nuns. Their father was, in simple lingo, a wife-beater. Somehow he ended up murdered, parts of his body found around the village. No one was ever charged. Their mother remarried and Pietro was considered their father.

"Yes," she said, "a grisly story, but with a happy ending for the women, praise God."

"Apparently four of them have."

I asked Sister if she intended to see a new movie, *The Color Purple,* based on Alice Walker's book. I thought it might be a good lens through which to view African American culture, one slice of life. She might well change her mind on the innocence of white Americans' nicknames for Blacks.

"If it's playing in Manhattan, I may find time to go see it."

We heard footsteps on the stairs, creaky as ever. I remembered how the steps used to bow down for Dad when he came upstairs at night to make sure we had knelt and said our prayers and blessed every last one of our family, no short task. Now it was Mom coming up to bring clean towels and linens for Sister Julieta. She came in and asked right away, "Sister Julieta, during your visits to my husband's cousin in Palermo, have you had a chance to visit the Black Madonna shrine in Tindari?"

"Oh yes, we went one day for a visit. You have to really want to get to that church. It is perched on a steep cliff. Very mystical."

"When I was in Sicily some years ago, we went there and also to the cave of Santa Rosalia where we had to enter on our knees. I loved the Black Madonna. You must have one or more in Kenya."

"Of course. We just call her Madonna."

We laughed. "That Tindari Madonna was carved in the 12th century," Mom said.

"You know the Bible refers to the words of the bride in the Song of Solomon, 'I am black but beautiful, O ye daughters of Jerusalem,' " Sister said. "Song of Solomon, chapter 1, verse 5." Then she recited the entire verse.

I am black but beautiful, O ye daughters of Jerusalem, as the tents of Cedar, as the curtains of Solomon. Do not consider me that I am brown, because the sun hath altered my color: the sons of my mother have fought against me, they have made me the keeper in the vineyards: my vineyard I have not kept.

After hearing it I understood the "but beautiful," which had seemed an odd compliment.

"Julieta," said Mom, "my husband has invited his friends Fletcher and Hampton to join us for dinner. They're eager to meet you. They're African Americans and one has a daughter at NYU, taking African studies."

"That sounds lovely. We'll have much to talk about."

"Rest now and I'll call you when supper, as we still call dinner here, is ready."

"*Amani,*" said Sister, palms together. "Peace."

"*Hakuna matata,*" I said.

Monday, November 18

ustomers were starting to request recipes for the many new varieties of fruits and vegetables showing up in the market. Dad reluctantly agreed to carry the unusual stuff. If it were up to the Italian customers, we'd carry only the items they've cooked forever, the various dark or bitter greens, eggplant, tomatoes, peppers, squashes, garlic, and onions.

Newly arrived immigrants from Latin and Mediterranean countries were finding Elizabeth an affordable place to live and work, especially if they commuted to New York. Their foodstuffs were starting to find shelf space in markets, along with the produce that many of America's various ethnic groups had already been eating for ages. Of course, America, the melting pot or stewpot, had always been adapting to the diet of its latest immigrants. But the 1980s seemed to be witnessing a food boom that was not possible before the confluence of jet-age transport of exotic ingredients and advances in refrigeration. Some food-scene observers gave credit for the diversifying American diet to the hippie backpack travelers of the 1960s and '70s who tramped the globe and brought back enlivened taste buds and recipes from afar.

Now a new type of customer was showing up and asking for produce they had read about in the popular food magazines, *Gourmet, Bon Appétit, Food & Wine,* and *Cook's Illustrated.* People called them young urban professionals or yuppies. Some were born-again or aging hippies who had moved on from a steady diet of sex, drugs, and rock'n'roll, and into the fast and affluent track of finance, business, and stock portfolios. Many were working on Wall Street or for ad agencies in midtown New York or for the big publishing empire—Time, Simon & Schuster, Random House, Fairchild, Knopf, and others. These nouveaux riches were finding Elizabeth, with its old wooden houses and aluminum-sided two-family buildings, not only cheap but a fast train or bus ride from New York City's Penn Station and Port Authority.

We had already done a demo for that younger segment on how to cook Italian greens. Now they were asking how to eat, and what to do with, the likes of star fruit, cherimoya, and prickly pear, which Mom said grew all over Sicily, where it was called *fico d'India.* Famous California chefs, starting to cook with our Italian staples, were having a strong influence on the New York culinary establishment. The East Coast food scene began introducing menu items such as broccoli rabe (sometimes called rapini), arugula (they called it roquette), and radicchio, an Italian chicory that looked like a Venetian sculpture.

Dad wondered aloud one day, "Maybe you and your sisters should make a trip into Manhattan and see what those newfangled, highfalutin greengrocers are up to." I talked to my brother Frankie and he offered to finance the trip. Rena was game to join me.

We decided not to ask the other sisters to come along because it would take all day to cover ground: As we remembered from our many past trips, the five of us together moved like a clumsy ten-legged sister-pede. I was coming from Mom and Dad's home so I met Rena at the Super Diner across from the Rahway train station. It was a cold day and I waited inside. To my surprise the old Greek owner, Adriana, greeted me with a smile and set down a free mug of terrible coffee, which I felt compelled to sip. I knew she had a tough reputation for throwing out customers she suspected of being on drugs. She was usually right.

"I knew your big sisters, Rena and the one who passed away," she said.

"Madeleine."

"Yes. They used to come here after school. Good girls. You all look alike."

"That had to be years ago," I said.

"I'm still here. Not even the dope addicts chase me away." I admired her chiseled facial bones and big black eyes, but she looked very tired.

I was grateful Rena appeared before I had to listen to more memories from before the time I had any of my own. Adriana and Rena chatted a few minutes about the good old days when Rahway teens had the Hullabaloo down the street.

"And the Cross Keys," reminisced Rena. "We all learned a line dance to 'Mustang Sally' there, before it burned down." Rena told Adriana she wished the kids today had places like that to hang out and dance—instead of heading into Manhattan and OD'ing on drugs and alcohol.

As Rena and I climbed the stairs to the train platform, Rena laughed and said how she had belonged to the party gangs who took advantage of New York's lower drinking age back in the day. "I survived those bad times, but I knew many
who didn't."

The express train to Penn Station gave her time to reminisce—I didn't mind this time—about a place she and her girlfriends used to go in the Village, the Red Witch. There they would drink a couple of beers, then stroll around the head shops buying peace signs on rawhide. On other weekends, if someone had a car they would drive "over the Island," as they called Staten Island, and drink Tom Collinses at Denino's or gin fizzes at the Red Lantern. Or they'd go over the Outerbridge Crossing to a place called the Orange House.

"Those were the days—we were invincible."

"You mean you're not anymore?"

I started to recall the places all we sisters had gone together over the years. It felt good to share memories I had been a part of. I remembered the Cloisters museum and garden, way up above Harlem. We were tempted but resisted picking herbs representing the monks of the Middle Ages. Some were edible, like chervil and fenugreek, some poisonous, like the deceptively pretty but deadly purple monkshood.

"You should tell Dad that people are starting to add flowers to salads—nasturtiums, forget-me-nots, and such," Rena said. "What'll they think of next?"

"Someone asked for fiddlehead ferns the other day," I said. "I read about them in a cookbook. Just one of the many new cuisine darlings." I recalled the passage:

> Cozy coils, kinetically poised, fiddleheads look like something about to slither across the produce counter. But the plumed lush green swirls are really inanimate shoots that have been plucked in their prime before they advance to a less gastronomically significant stage.

The author went on to say that *fiddlehead* referred to the way the fronds coiled, a pattern more technically known as *circinate vernation*.

We were adventurous when it came to food but still we held our tried-and-true dishes in high esteem. Rena recalled a sister trip we made one weekend to Harlem. We ate barbecued ribs, grits, and a mess of greens at Sylvia's, run by the soul food maven, then danced the night away at the Cotton Club. We tried to get Mom and Dad to come with us. But they felt their nightclub days were over, though they had very good memories, especially of the night they met up at the St. Francis Cabrini shrine over the Hudson.

Rena said, "Dad told me when he meets people from New York they say they're from New Jersey because it has a better reputation."

"The Garden State has a nice ring," I said, "better than the Empire State."

We recalled the many times we'd gone to the theater district. Most recently we took Mom and Dad to see Duke Ellington's *Sophisticated Ladies*. We ate rack of lamb and chocolate soufflé at Sardi's and loved looking at all the caricatures of famous stage and screen actors.

Rena remembered how in the late '70s she had finally gone to see *Hair* with her girlfriends. "In those days we ate spaghetti and drank true dago red at Enrico & Paglieri, kind of a latter-day Mama Leone's all-you-can-eat."

"How about the time we splurged at the Plaza's Champagne Bar for our group birthday celebration?" I said.

"I loved it—no wonder Hemingway told Fitzgerald to give his liver to Princeton and his heart to the Plaza. At least that's the story, apocryphal or not."

"*A pocket full of* story can go a long, long way for a long, long time," I said, thinking about the Last Cannoli. "Hey, remember the hunter from Alaska we met at the bar?"

"He kept asking if we knew when open season was for black bear. He looked like a bear," Rena said.

"He'd come all the way from Alaska to get an East Coast black bear. Said it was different from those in the Northwest. Which he said tasted like ham. Go figure."

"I think he was there as someone's guest, not your run-of-the-mill Champagne Bar patron. I noticed he was drinking . . . furnaces?"

"Boilermakers," Rena said.

"That. I remember afterward we went to Elaine's, all five of us, and the bill was only a little more than our drink tab at the Plaza."

"Was that the same night we waited in line at Michael's Pub for Woody Allen to come in and play his sax?"

"Clarinet. No, that was another time . . . I think we ate at Tavern on the Green."

"Too many out-of-towners there."

Before the train pulled into Penn Station we had time to recall visits to a friend on West 96th who took us walking through Central Park around the reservoir. We saw the Dakota where John Lennon had lived with Yoko Ono and their son. We were still smarting from John's assassination. We wondered if Mayor Koch was letting Manhattan get too touristy. We decided to save our long stroll down Fifth Avenue for after Thanksgiving, tourists be damned. We loved the festive showcases of Herald Square with their hundreds of colored Christmas lights and mechanical toys, marionettes, trains, life-size dolls. Macy's, Saks, Bergdorf, Bloomingdale's—all outdid each other every Yuletide in the most mesmerizing wonderland for kids of all ages.

We would be doing most of our research in lower Manhattan this trip. We regretted not having time to stop at the Silver Palate with its astonishing array of salads and deli foods. Where would we eat? We entertained the idea of dining at either Il Cortile on Mulberry Street, or at a Chinese restaurant Rena's friend Guy Yo had once taken us to, the 4-5-6 on Mott Street. But those were places best for a crowd, say with all five of the sisters. We took a subway down to the Cupping Room on West Broadway where we could enjoy a light brunch and consider our plan of attack. Years ago we had started a sister ritual of going there in elegant millinery like 1940s ladies. We loved the daintiness of the place as well as their strong brews and home-baked pastries. It called for fashion statements like our fancy vintage headgear.

On our way we stopped first at Balducci's, the nearby greengrocer that also sold meat, fish, and deli goods. One of the owners, Luigi, knew our dad because they spoke the same tongue, whether Sicilian or produce. I made note of the unusual items the market was carrying, including a dark red *cicoria* and several different types of eggplant. Dad only carried the male and female ones, I told Luigi. He shook his head and rolled his eyes as if that were an old Italian wives' tale.

For the life of me, I couldn't figure out why they were importing broccoli rabe, when back in the Garden State we easily found it grown. I asked Luigi and he said they were only importing the seeds. I told him where Dad got it in New Jersey and he was thankful for the tip. Just to be nice, I bought a bottle of their imported extra-virgin olive oil, although Mom and Dad still liked the big tins of Gemma and Progresso brands. I noticed they were carrying a California brand of extra-virgin. I couldn't imagine it could compete with Europe's thousand-year-old tradition.

We strolled slowly past the dizzying array of old and new items. At the bulb fennel, I told Rena the story of Frankie and the finocchio in San Francisco, and how he searched all over the city for *god-dunes* but never found any, only a male eggplant. Balducci, we saw, carried *god-dunes*. They looked domestic, not wild, which meant less oomph or flavor. They were too sterile looking. I didn't tell Luigi. Come to think of it, a lot of his produce was sterile looking. Sour grapes maybe, but I figured long after people got tired of the wild out-there items, they'd settle back to eating the standards.

We took our break at the Cupping Room, then went on to Dean & DeLuca. Following their example, I decided we should carry more of the exotic mushrooms, not just porcini and morels. I paged through a copy of *The Silver Palate Cookbook* and an intriguing but lesser-known book called *The New & Exotic Foods*. I made note of the latter's recipes to share with our more adventurous customers:

Arugula with chanterelles and toasted walnuts
Amaranth greens with sweet-and-sour bacon dressing
Boniato with maple buttermilk dressing
Breadfruit soup
Celeriac with mustard cream dressing
Home-fried chayote with rosemary
Fiddlehead ferns with porcini cream
Jerusalem artichokes au gratin
Kabocha with lime-coriander sauce
Kohlrabi and ham patties
Pomelo and avocado salad
Golden puree of rutabaga
Radicchio, eggplant, and rice salad
Poached salmon with tarragon-chervil

By the time I had written them all down in quick shorthand, Rena and I were exhausted, overloaded with food visions. It was too late for lunch, too early for dinner. But that wouldn't stop us from having small bites somewhere.

We decided to kill time waiting for Sweet Basil Jazz Club on Seventh Avenue South to open. There we'd catch one of our favorite jazz musicians, Doc Cheatham, whom we had met on several occasions. He was the kindest gentleman and always remembered who we were. "The Jersey Girls," he called us.

We called Vinnie and Dana, who lived on West Broadway. They agreed to meet us at Sweet Basil in the evening. They were excited that Frankie Manning, the famous Lindy Hopper known as the Swing King, was coming to offer a workshop at their dance studio. They'd found a 1941 film in the New York Film archives, *Hellzapoppin'*, with Frankie kicking up an inferno. "Dad used to see him at the Savoy Ballroom in Harlem—that's where he learned his shim-sham," Vinnie told us. "Frankie is 71 and moves like a teenage pup on uppers. He's the Energizer Bunny of dance." Only problem, they said, was that Frankie would draw such a huge crowd, their studio might be too small. I thought, but didn't say, *Someday we'll have a mansion down Elizabethport where we'll have wooden dance floors to spare.*

We made our way slowly on foot to MacDougal near Bleecker and found a table at Caffe Reggio, one of the few businesses to serve a real cannoli. We ordered one, with two cappuccinos, and put it in the center of the table. I said a prayer to Madeleine before we shared it.

"To Serpico, too," Rena said. "Wherever he is."

"To Al Pacino, wherever he is," I said.

Two tourists came in and sat near our table. They asked what we were eating. We told them and they wanted to know if it was good.

"Nah," said Rena. We could tell they did not believe her.

"We'll have what she's having and not enjoying," they told the waiter.

"You think it was their Last Cannoli?" I asked Rena.

"Nah," Rena said as she nibbled a bite, "we are the only ones in the world to have a Last Cannoli."

"Right on, sister," I said savoring that incomparable pudding-sweet, cheesy, creamy filling. "God forbid it should go mainstream."

"Fat chance."

Tuesday, November 19

"**I** bet Mark Twain slept here," Rena said. My sisters and I stood at the perimeter of the Mariners Mansion down the Port, once a busy waterway, still somewhat so. In the distance, white clouds of steam or smoke rose from some industry, its pollutants reined in by new environmental regulations.

"Really?" asked Lucy.

"Don't be so gullible," I said. "If Twain slept here so did Washington, Elvis, and Marilyn."

"Really?"

"And whoever else comes to mind who made the rounds—and is still making the rounds as a restless spirit."

"But never the *twains* shall meet," Rena said.

I told them, "We do know that ship men slept here. The extravagant home was built in the late 1800s by a wealthy ship captain. I forget his name—"

"Maybe it was James Cook," Maria said.

"That was Hawaii," Teresa said.

"The name of the Indians," I explained, "was the Lenape,

from whom the land that became Elizabethtown was quote-unquote 'purchased.' One can only imagine for what or how much."

"Twenty-four bucks in wampum, package deal with Manhattan," Rena said.

"Yep, the Lenape, Manhattan, some Dutch guy named Peter, likely where Peterstown comes from . . . or was that a German Peter. Anyway, apparently a Captain Philip Carteret arrived at the Arthur Kill area where the white settlers had already procured the land and he called it Elizabethtown after his cousin Elizabeth. Use your imagination to see the meadows and wetlands that were once here. Blot out the smokestacks."

"The Mariners Mansion, I like the sound of it," said Maria.

"If we ever get hold of it, let's keep that name," said Teresa.

"After the captain died and his family sold the mansion, it was many things including a town hall, an orphanage, and, if you believe urban myths, briefly a bordello for sailors. Currently it's a haunted house—which is a euphemism meaning a hangout for teens who want to smoke, drink, and indulge in other vices."

"Let's case the joint," Rena said.

"Let's stroll the grounds first," I said, "make sure the juveniles aren't here. Dad scared them away last time."

"He has a way," said Lucy.

"Don't we all know," I said.

Since I had gone to the library and looked up details, I was able to tell them how the 1889 mansion displayed a variety of architectures that were popular during the late 19th century. Its exterior was mostly brick and stone—perhaps quarried stone. It also retained some of the popular Federal style from the previous century.

"In the late 1800s, architects were inspired by historical styles, including Gothic Revival, Queen Anne, and Renaissance Revival. This shows in the mansion's ornate façade, with its highly decorative and intricate carvings, moldings, and the stately turrets, towers, and dormers."

"It must be hard to find curved glass to replace those round windows in the tower."

"Yes, but a few places make it to order—I checked."

We marveled at a porch or portico with columns, the symmetrical façade with its evenly spaced windows and doors.

"Those are called Palladian windows—a large central window with two smaller windows on either side—a popular feature of the Federal style."

"Love the way they arch."

"Look at this entryway!" they all exclaimed.

"Many mansions of those eras had this sort of opulent entry. Note the central doorway flanked by two columns or pilasters. Don't you love this grand entrance?" I prodded. I wanted to light a fire of support for Dad. "Think back to those old movies like *The Leopard* with Burt Lancaster. The entrance of a late-19th-century mansion, whether here or in Palermo, was often a big affair."

"*Madon'*, look at this huge carved door," Rena said. We ran our hands over it and felt transported back to 1889. Inside we marveled at ornate ironwork, carved wood details, and decorative plasterwork. We found the spacious asymmetrical floor plan I had read about; rooms seemed to occur in a haphazard way, creating an interesting, if whimsical, layout. Our thousand-square-foot Cape Cod home could have fit inside more than five times.

We felt the long-gone past, the calcified memories, deeds and misdeeds, secrets shameful and boastful. The lives of crumbled affluence. All of it a buck away from being ours to do with what we pleased. Well, there was a catch.

"The high ceilings are a mark of luxury and grandeur," I said, playing tour guide and curator for this run-down structure. "And watch for falling paint chips." I pointed out chair rails and cornices.

"Chair rail? I thought that was called wainscoting," said Lucy.

"A chair rail molding is carved from wood, clean cut and streamlined, classic and sophisticated," I quoted my source.

"You'd hardly gather that from this. Guess you have to look past the deterioration," said Rena.

"Today the chair rail is a decorative element but back then it was to protect walls from chairs and other furniture. It actually dates back to the Greeks and Romans, who were always concerned with visual proportions," I said.

"Everything goes back to Greeks or Romans," Lucy said. "Even us, it seems. Mom said Sicily had more Greek ruins than Greece. It was once part of Magna Graecia."

"Now wainscoting," I continued, "is paneling, usually of wood, but could also be pressed tin. It wraps around the room in an attempt to add depth to the space. We can see an example upstairs on the second floor."

We made our way through dining rooms with built-in china cabinets, living rooms, long halls, and three stairwells. A mudroom out back led to the garden. We imagined the kitchen's built-in cupboards filled with sturdy and fine china. The ceiling in one dining room looked like a game board with its wells between wooden beams.

"This looks like the room where Colonel Mustard murdered Miss Scarlet with the candelabra," said Maria.

"What was your first clue?" asked Rena.

"You sure it wasn't the other way around?" said Teresa.

"No, I think it was Mark Twain," piped Lucy.

"Whoever," I said. "There used to be gorgeous glass or crystal chandeliers but they've been looted. As have the toilets and bidets. Some sinks remain."

"Bidets?" said Lucy. "That captain was certainly not American. Americans still don't get the bidet's benefits."

"Too prudish," I said.

"So much work would need to be done to make this mansion livable," Rena said. "Is it worth it?"

Even as we marveled at the decorative interior details, we gingerly stepped through plaster and paint chips and droppings.

"It takes a keen eye," Lucy said, "to imagine these fireplace mantels cleaned up and restored. How many are there?"

"At least three as I recall. And look at that stained glass window—the geometric shapes. The positioning to let natural light in at high noon," I said, though I only made up that last part.

We saw the fixtures where gas once lighted the mansion.

"Let's see, if our home once slept 12, this joint could easily sleep maybe 50 kids. Think of the slumber parties!"

"But Dad only wants ten to start. He wants them to have the space he could not give his first ten, and other good stuff."

The Mariners Mansion was close to the Port, where heavy industry had grown up around it. It was one of those unicorn historic buildings that managed to stay standing even as an industrial society closed in on it. Its days were numbered if someone didn't come up with a buck and a promise of some grand amount. It had become arthritic to some extent—its pipes and wires decrepit and going to shambles. But it had a sturdy skeleton otherwise. Good vibes, too, we noted. You can't buy or build good vibes. That was because it had history, tradition, and still stood proudly. It was surrounded by a lot of land, considering the density of the city, and even a few trees that had been there since at least the 1800s. When I last came here with my father I had seen passionately burning embers of coal in his eyes, flashing lasers of white-hot light, in the way I saw gemstones in the eyes of my sisters. I felt more and more clairvoyant. Maybe it was sparks of the fire Dad had to tamp down to go to war, to raise ten children. *There will be a way.* Maybe that was what Madeleine was trying to tell me in my dreams. Day dreams, night dreams, I believed in them.

After a good two hours of sizing up the interior we headed to Caffe Italia in Peterstown, where we could make like Dad and let rip our own dreams about the Mariners Mansion.

Wednesday, November 20

Like a textbook criminal I returned to the scene of the crime. I parked a few blocks from the Villa Roma just in case my father surprised me and came by. More likely, he'd be at his produce business working till early this evening.

Big Frank, a regular fixture at the semidark bar, didn't see me at first. I noticed that he looked worn out. Flabby from the back. Pear-shaped. He wore a white short-sleeve shirt and black pants. His frizzed black hair bobbed over the cash register, betraying the Sicilian streak of African blood.

A few happy hour barflies were talking loudly about the recent World Series. I supposed that Royals and Cardinals were baseball teams, not ruling families or bird species, which would have interested me much more. I gathered it was an edge-of-seat win by the Royals. But beyond that it was a foreign language with jargon that escaped me. I had to think what the ball looked like—round, hard, fitting the palm. Not oval or big as an orange globe.

I sat at the same round table as at my last visit with Dad, unnoticed in a dark corner. This gave me time to ruminate. What would I say to Frank? I looked around the empty wood floor and stage and my 3-D memory replayed the weddings I'd attended here. First Lucy, then Mario, Vinnie, and Carmine had had their wedding receptions in this hall. I was only five when Lucy got married but that day was one of the most exciting in my short life, the biggest fanfare I had ever witnessed. Lucy had three bridesmaids, including her maid of honor. I had never seen such gorgeous fabric, satin and chiffon, in a color I knew today as teal, the most appealing blend of blue and green, second in beauty only to periwinkle blue in my mind.

True to my nickname, I had moved like an unseen cat around the rooms where Lucy and her wedding party slipped into their lacy undergarments and gowns. I could still hear the crisp swish of crinolines. They all wore chunky two-inch satin heels dyed matching teal. Their perfume filled the air. Something by Prince Matchabelli, or was it My Sin by Lanvin? Or Emeraude? All three, I think.

For days, Lucy, Mom, and Rena had folded pink and white tissue into gowns for dolls that were fastened to cars' prows in the bridal motorcade along with streamers of crepe paper. The groom and his friends, in tuxedos with carnations in their lapels, were out of a storybook too. The flowers—bouquets everywhere from the church to the park, where they took endless photos, to the Villa Roma, where the band had started and the wedding party were introduced one couple at a time. What was Lucy and Joe's song? I couldn't recall. There was the dancing, from rock to the tarantella to ballroom for the parents. The bride throwing her bouquet, removing her garter to pass to the next hopeful maiden— all ran through my mind now like a three-act play by Chekhov or a scene in a Coppola film.

After Lucy's wedding, I was jaded. Nothing would ever be as grand, I thought. The following weddings were never quite as magnificent. It was only many years later I learned how expensive those affairs were. I can't say I ever hoped to be that sort of star attraction, although I believed that vows of love eternal were worthy endeavors. My pet retort to my aunts, who often asked when they would dance at my wedding, was the famous Gloria Steinem (or was it Dorothy Parker?) quote: "I can't mate in captivity." Which, to my delight, drove them crazy.

Big Frank saw me and wandered over to my table. "Hey, *ch' se dic*? Where's *tuo padre*?" He placed a shot glass of anisette in front of me. He knew I loved the licorice flavor. I sipped it as slowly as I could, though I wanted to throw it back and feel that glowing warm effect.

"He's working, Big Frank," I said. "I'll cut to the chase." But then how to start? Really, what could Frank do?

"What? Something bad happen?" He looked frightened, so I said no, nothing new or bad.

"I'm not supposed to know about the hot merchandise that bozo Sammy Bono is storing at my father's business. But I do."

"Carmela, look, I wouldn't worry. Let things cool. There's things you don't know."

"I know what I don't know," I said testily. "My father needs to be clear of any criminal activity. He has a dream to buy the old Mariners Mansion for a buck."

"*Madon'*, your father!"

"He'll need a lot of do-re-mi," I said, trying to speak Big Frank's lingo.

"Let me show you something." Frank rolled up the shirt cuff on his right arm. There was a perfect black band like a bruise all around his wrist.

"What happened?"

"Remember that watch Bono threw at your father—the one they played catch with?"

"Yes."

"Hold on, I'll be back in a sec." He went behind the bar and came back with the watch. The gold band was tarnished but the face was surrounded by the small jewels of my sisters' eyes—sapphire, ruby, emerald, topaz, and amethyst.

"*Mama mia*, it's beautiful except for the tarnished band," I said.

"Read the brand name on the face."

I looked at the small sans serif letters and saw a familiar name. "Rolex?"

"Look again," he said. I did and this time I noticed the E looked broken off, more like a C.

"It's a knockoff. Those are glass stones," Frank said. "Which is not to say the ones he wants stored at your Dad's—bite my tongue—are not genuine. Who knows. I wore it for a day, forgot to take it off in the shower. That's what I get, tarnished wrist for my arrogance."

Then I noticed that the Roman numeral for four was

shown as IV—the gauche way, according to Mario, for expensive watches. "It's all so confusing. Well, I'll be on my way. Would you please not tell my father I've been here?"

"Mum's the word, or as we Sicilians say, *omerta*. You might want to talk to Ralph Giordano—maybe he can give you some reassurance about the land your father's business is on."

"He's in jail."

"Oh yeah, I forgot . . . As safe a place as any for you to talk to him."

Wednesday Evening, November 20

When I talked to Lucy about my dream, she first thought Madeleine was confirming that repressed libido can Kill.

Or at least my subconscious that produced the dream believed so. Lucy and her psych textbooks. We all loved to hear the symbolism beneath the surface of our dream and waking lives, even if it didn't always resonate with our take on reality. We then alluded to Dad's inability to forgive himself and concluded how guilt can also shorten life span. Oh, we were such decipherers of family psychology and mythology, we the sisterhood.

Lucy, like our mother, had had a quantum awakening. Both occurred after painful events. And both women never seemed happier. Lucy was back with Joe after three years apart—after the four children, when the Other Woman was out of the picture. Mom never had the luxury of separation after Dad's Other Woman episode—until she went to Sicily. Now we had heard the depth of her visit. My sisters and I were still marveling at how LouAnn, the bobbed blond Mom had mistaken for the Other Woman come to beg her forgiveness, was now her best friend. Lucy got her therapist's license and riddled out these relationships in her own way. She tossed around the names of Freud, Jung, Maslow, Lacan like they were rock stars.

Lucy, Rena, Maria, Teresa, and I had gathered again at Grandma Coniglio's, ostensibly to check on Grandma. Grandma did not want to move to a nursing home, although she'd had a couple of falling scares. We were trying to accommodate her with frequent visits. Grandma and Grandpa, when he was alive, were your classic Italians from the Old World who came, put down roots, and refused to move, America's mobile society be damned. Despite the encroaching air and water pollution of Elizabeth, with its Superfund sites and Brownfields, our grandparents managed to live to a ripe old age without serious health repercussions. Fanciful as it was, I imagined their home encircled in neutral turf, a tidy bell jar like the bubble encasing Mom's garden in Rahway—a sort of environmental demilitarized zone where damaging free radicals never penetrated. Perhaps the one peach tree and the small vegetable garden were equivalent to guards, gatekeepers, letting pass through only wholesome antioxidants.

Grandma set out her crusty bread, sweet butter, home-cured olives, salami, roasted peppers, and provolone. Lucy was talking about some of the patients she was shepherding through their love crises. She fascinated us by describing what she called their ego chalice (her hands forming a malleable basket) as rigid or weak. "It breaks when the light of images surges into it. Psychosis, the void, can overwhelm."

Unlike Mom, Lucy had made her situation more symmetrical, more balanced, by taking a lover—at least for a while, until she found joy within. "I am a joy magnet," she now boasted. She'd been cracked open and found oodles of joyfulness in and around her life, her kids, her family, her husband, her day-to-day routine, even when it was monotonous. There was boundless joy. Her arms stretched wide. It seemed very similar to Mom's epiphany in Sicily, which we keep learning about only in small increments. Which goes to show one can be reborn or born again anywhere, anytime, anyway.

Lucy said that during her dark period she didn't want to indulge what her fellow Jungian psychologists called the crucifix conflict. Her arms opened and spread again: "People feel martyred, hung on the cross. Some women—or men— resolve the conflict by cutting off one side of the crucifix. Or they stay with it and see what comes. They integrate, move through, go forward. Love the self through the conflict." She raised her arms together overhead in contrast to the crucifix.

"They choose to embrace the energy that arises in the face of their men's old girlfriends, wives, lovers." With her palms she made an image of uniting them. "They ally themselves as friend, sister, confidant. Becoming one, but keeping their identity. Rather than letting the jealous inner woman come forth to polarize and cause pain for all."

We listened to Lucy, transfixed, but still able to nosh on Grandma's spread. "Maybe our mother, devout Catholic that she is, discovered that the Black Madonna she saw in Tindari is more like the goddess of light. God the Father may be the spirit."

"Black Madonna, I read about her in Doris Lessing's *African Stories*," Maria said.

"Me too," said Teresa.

"The Black Madonna journeyed through Sicily," Lucy continued. "Her route was like the Silk Road, following the trajectory of least resistance. Many Christians cannot accept her pigment. She's been bleached in places, not just her pigment but her wholeness. She was wife, mother, erotic woman; all selves are possible with her. So I can be sensual, nurturer, caregiver to men/children. At the same time I can be cerebral, intellectual lover of ideas, achiever, and honor my masculine/compulsive side. Not so in the dichotomy of many cultures. Sisters, we did not grow up with all these role models, we have integrated them ourselves through feminine wisdom."

"Amen, amen," Rena said. "Say it loud."

"Now you are integrated at the ripe old age of 40," I said to Lucy.

"Forty-one. Unlike the Blessed Virgin Mary," she said, "who had no sexuality, that is she was cut off from it—a full

sex-ectomy. So in our culture, man has his wife and children and his lust goes to the Other Woman. But the Black Madonna incorporates all aspects of being female."

Madeleine, if you are listening, I hope you are learning this in your afterlife.

"Another important theme that I shepherd my clients through," said Lucy, "is trust, faith. When images are crazy, confusing, scary, I help them stay open and trust. Surrender. This theme appears over and over in Twelve Step programs, Zen Buddhism, Christianity, other faiths."

Grandma came down the hallway into the kitchen to ask what else we wanted to eat. It occurred to me that she, one hell of a designated fussy woman with sensual hips and voluptuous bosom, had been influenced by the Black Madonna paradigm, consciously or not. She would never tell. We said we needed no more food, made sure she was okay, and hugged her good-bye.

We went to Caffe Italia again. On the way there I thought about how all the dark episodes were behind our family and we were cruising. Except for that nagging potentially dark episode with Sammy Bono. I let it rest.

Thursday, November 21

"Not a spoon of dirt is bulldozed that we don't got a piece of," said Ricardo Bracchi, the powerful labor union leader.

I was reading the Newark *Star-Ledger*, the morning paper, still looking for any mention of stolen watches. I had been scanning the news every morning since that day Sammy Bono strong-armed my father into storing his cache of hot merchandise somewhere on the premises of Dad's produce business.

I read quickly through the news du jour, mostly of marginal interest to me. The Live Aid concert was still being equally praised and assessed for its effectiveness. Impresario Bob Geldof was quoted frequently for his assertion that rock was now the lingua franca of the concept of one world. Coca-Cola—a drink which almost never appeared in my childhood home—was introducing the New Coke. The sinking of the Greenpeace ship *Rainbow Warrior* was still being investigated. French agents had been implicated but there was no proof yet. Michael Jordan was named NBA Rookie of the Year.

I was also checking the police blotter whenever it appeared in the local news. Car theft, gas station robberies, high-speed chases, pockets picked; voyeurism, exhibitionsm, myriad other sex crimes; attempted kidnapping; drug possession; trespass on a rusty old freighter in Secaucus; assault with a potentially deadly weapon (oversized zucchini).

Nothing about watches.

The predominant strain of local mob activity was orchestrated by Bracchi. He was considered New Jersey's indigenous mobster, accused of racketeering and extortion and essentially running the construction industry, Local 369, with an iron fist. He was still being investigated and had somehow eluded conviction so far. But his day would likely come. People said he probably got away with murder—literally and figuratively—because he gave so generously to the Police Athletic League and to Elizabeth and Newark youth programs. It crossed my mind to approach this Bracchi, a fellow Italian, for help getting the Mariners Mansion. I had heard that Dad's buddy Ralph Giordano had ties to Bracchi. As sure as I was that my father was a God-fearing, lawful, and upright citizen, I knew that he also knew the workings of this underworld. Things he would never speak aloud or share.

Everyone knew the secret hiding in plain sight—that Bracchi was a close associate of Sam the Plumber, one Simone DeCavalcante, the biggest mob boss born on Jersey soil. If he didn't like someone he had them rubbed out.

I had already gone to visit Ralph Giordano in the Union County jail. He was surprised but glad to see me. I made him promise not to tell my father. No problem. He couldn't tell me what he was accused of but seemed to think he'd be getting out soon. He had a hearing coming up and he had a good lawyer.

"It's all a mistake, case of mistaken identity. But it's cozy here, so no complaints." I had surmised from Sammy and Big Frank that Ralph also felt safer being incarcerated. His sons were taking care of his auto body repair business on Route 1 in Elizabeth.

I told Ralph about the watches and that brought an odd snicker. "Watches! My right eye." That's all he would say. Ralph explained what I now knew, that until recently he had owned the land where Dad had his produce business. The prime location had allowed my father to build a bigger stand with a sturdy galvanized roof, covered for winter and inclement weather.

"But you see, I didn't expect to cause your father, my goombah for chrissakes, any trouble. Sammy. . . I can't tell you all the details." He cleared his throat and lowered his voice. "I had to deed the land to Sammy. At least till I can buy it back." He said a few other things, more or less coded. Like when I asked if he was lonely for more visitors, he said, "Nah, they might want to bring me some home-baked bread or cake that would give me a fatal case of indigestion." I thought of the funny movies where a knife or gun was baked into the bread or cake.

Things didn't become clear as I listened to Ralph, but at least they were less foggy. "He's got me over a barrel," Dad had said. A barrel. I tried to recall if Dad had any barrels around the business.

Ralph was going on with old stories that had a statute of limitations built in. "If the walls at Spirito's pizzeria only had ears. Your father coulda been a driver during Prohibition, they wanted to cut him in. He'da been on easy street the rest of his life. But always looking over his shoulder. Know what I mean? Then there was them bootleggers from Newark asked to store some barrels of flour in his father's cellar. His father, Mario Donitella, God bless him, looked the other way and never asked questions. Your father got his upstanding ways from your grandfather."

"I wish he hadn't died before any of his grandkids were born."

Ralph went on, "Sometimes the most important thing is that one hand washes the other." Where had I heard that before? "Your grandfather never took the easy way. He never sat on his behind and let the American government take care of him. Not from the day he stepped off the boat and put his foot on American soil. He worked his *cahunas* off. Did you know he sold hay, oats, coal, bought the horse and buggy with his life savings. The people in Peterstown knew him as *il C'rabonari* when he delivered the coal. He learned English, sold insurance to Italians in Peterstown. He turned down a job as supervisor at the Prudential because that Irishman Burns told him, 'There's no room for your kind up here.' But he made ends meet and took care of 16 cousins, aunts, uncles. That was my goombah's father."

I loved these stories, embroidered or not. What did it matter? I told Ralph about the Mariners Mansion Dad wanted to purchase for one dollar, but needed to commit $50,000 to renovating over the next two years. Ralph visibly held back tears and said, "For all his earthly ways, your father is a walking saint. I bet he never told you kids how he sent the cloth to Sicily for his cousin's fiancée's wedding gown back in 1949. Things were dirt-poor in Sicily after the war. Shirt off his back? I seen him do it more than once. So he was a bit edgy when he came home from the war. Who wasn't? You carry those demons for life. You simply keep them at bay, in limbo. Or wherever. We all drank too much at first when we got home. It was our homegrown therapy. I know some of the guys didn't recover from it. But those of us who did, we are here . . . like my goombah, your dad . . . to make the crazy world a better place."

I told Ralph he was good people, no matter what the law said or did. He teared up again and tried to reach across the barricade to hug me. *"Stai bene, cara mia."* Before he was led away he told me again sotto voce, though I'm sure the guards could hear, "Why don't you go to one of your dad's *goombahs* twice removed, Ricardo Bracchi. Ask him for a grant. He's pretty generous with causes for kids." Ralph was gone before I could yell back, "Are you nuts?! My father would never accept tainted money from a mobster." Okay, okay, so I did very briefly consider going that route and accepting the money myself.

It was not the first time I really thought about my father

as not fully formed, but someone who might have changed and grown, especially because of, or in spite of, the war. My sisters recalled to me his reaction to the 1969 Kent State killings. He was a bona fide hawk until that day. Now he was not a dove, but he no longer believed every war that the United States of America got into was right and just.

Checking the newspapers later I read that Salvatore Enrico Bono had been arrested and was being held without bail on felony charges. Suspicion of trafficking in hot merchandise.

Friday, November 22

I t baffled me that the news account of Sammy's arrest did not say a word about watches. But it also put my mind somewhat at ease, for the time being. As I drove, I saw a bumper sticker reading PLAY THE ACCORDION, GO TO JAIL—IT'S THE LAW. It struck me as funny because I was going to prison. I loved the accordion. Cousin Bernie often played it at weddings and other family affairs.

The outside of the prison was dark red, blood amber brick with a signature black dome on one part of the complex. All the times we'd driven by here on our way to the country, I never imagined I'd set foot inside.

After I had gone through security and showed my ID a guard approached me. "Can I help you?" he asked gruffly.

I took a deep breath. "I'm here to see someone . . . um . . . Sammy Bono. He's in here for breaking a law." *Not for playing the accordion*, I thought.

The guard's face almost cracked a smile, and his expression softened. "Sit in this waiting room, I'll be right back."

"Where are you going?" I must have sounded shrill.

"Going to speak to the warden. Be patient. The name was?"

"Salvatore Bono—Salvatore Enrico Bono."

"Humph, a mouthful. Just wait here."

As I waited what seemed an interminably long time between walls painted a depressingly insipid tan, I watched inmates come and go in their regulation powder-blue shirts and dark trousers, work boots or sneakers. Most were Black or brown men. Some could have been Italian or Hispanic. Some inmates were handcuffed and led by guards. Some were burly, scary looking, others looked like college professors with wire-rimmed glasses, still others were buff and athletic, but harmless looking.

Eventually the guard returned and said, "I'm sorry, but you can't see Mr. Bono."

I felt a surge of frustration. For weeks now I'd wanted to put an end to having the stolen merchandise stashed somewhere at my father's clean produce business. I was getting tired of dead ends. So what came out of my mouth was, "But he's my husband, well my former, we're still friends. I just want to visit for a few minutes. Please?"

The guard grimaced. "I'm afraid that won't be possible."

I let out an exasperated sound and was about to scream at the guard. He raised his hand with a sort of sad look and said, "You can't see him because he's dead."

For a minute I was speechless. "What? How? Where's the body?"

"Body's been taken to the prison morgue. There'll be an autopsy to determine cause of death. So sorry, ma'am."

I knew it was futile to keep pressing the guard, who seemed sincere. I had a friend whose husband briefly worked at this prison. He had been horrified by the routine strip searches and the prevailing inhumanity among both guards and prisoners. He quit after a month and took a lower-paying job in a health food store.

I began to cry, certainly not for Sammy, but for all the frustration of the past weeks coming to a head. I had hoped this would be resolved by Thanksgiving. "Can't you tell me anything more?"

"Sorry, ma'am, I don't have any more details."

I forced a thank-you to the guard and turned to leave. He escorted me to the gate, then said in a low voice, "Mrs. Bono—okay, I know you're not his wife, ex or whatever."

"How do you know that?"

"His *other* wife came and she looked the part—teased black hair and face paint. You ain't never been married to that slime-bag Bono, pardon my crudeness. Anyway, Mr. Bono had a couple of visitors yesterday. I don't know who they were, but they looked like thugs. And there was a lot of tension between them—just saying, you know stress can bring on cardiac failure."

"Right." I took it in, not sure why he was telling me this. "Thank you for that." Then I thought of something. "Did one of them have a deep scar on his left cheek?"

The guard slowly nodded.

As I drove home to my pad on Roselle Street in Linden,

I felt two things. One was a sense of guilt. I had wished for Sammy's death, even prayed for him to die and go to hell. Of course, I didn't believe I had the power to cause his death. Tears of despair were streaming down my face as I couldn't help but think the guard meant to signal me that the two visitors had something to do with Sam's death. But what? I didn't need to know the truth about what had happened to Sam, only to get the stash of hot timepieces out of our lives.

Saturday, November 23

"**A**re we not susceptible to a sort of mob psychology?" Lucy was speculating more than seeking a hard answer. This afternoon we were sitting on her porch in Bradley Beach. I could hear the ocean a block away, its winter sound track like smooth jazz, a low bluesy jam, content to have broad sand beaches to roll upon. Tourists had been gone since Labor Day. Lucy was riffing on some behavioral text she had been reading.

"Sister Mob Psyche 101," Rena said idly. None of us was sure where the discussion was headed but Lucy always introduced engaging new perspectives on family dynamics.

"True, we've been forged in the sister crucible," Lucy said.

My mind drifted like wood on a calm swell. I was forever considering the double-edged blessing and bane of the timepieces. If I could find them, if I could sell them, for how much, how many were there . . . It sounded like dozens, each worth close to a thousand, two thousand bucks times three dozen . . . numbers, numbers, numbers. The numbing effect of them. Something resonated in the phrase *sister mob*. I thought of how we had already used Mafia tactics once, in a way. It interrupted my stream of consciousness as I recalled a scene from about three years ago.

I asked my sisters, "Do you remember Stella's stalker?" Stella was a close friend of Maria and Teresa's. The guy kept on bugging Stella, showing up wherever she went—didn't understand *no*—until she was afraid to step out her front door.

"Was he the one we made cry?" Lucy asked.

"He might have cried but not in front of us," said Maria.

"He's the one. We had Stella sleep at our apartment and we held his dog hostage," said Teresa.

"It was mean," I said. "But it got him to abide by the bogus restraining order."

"Right. You can thank Chester, our cop friend I was dating, for that," said Teresa.

"Dude was too dumb to know a forged document," said Rena. "Good ol' Chester, he agreed it was best we work under the radar—because of the dognapping."

"Okay," I said, "it was the mutt, then, who whined pitifully for its master. Who was the other perv we made sob?"

"That was the guy who flashed us in the park when we were jogging," Rena said.

"What was he thinking, that the five of us would applaud?" Maria asked.

"Four of you," Teresa said. "I wasn't there that time. But I did go to night court with you."

I cringed as I recalled the details. "We really tortured that creep," I said.

"I can still hear his voice trembling as he begged us to 'let me put my dick back in my pants,' " said Maria. I was one of the three holding his arms nearly out of their sockets. We sat on his legs, belittling his penis with every insult we could pull out of our billed caps. After we managed to get the ID from his wallet we let him repack his penis.

"Maybe we went too far," I said.

"He got off easy with the plea bargaining," Rena said.

"I guess we were thinking of the adolescent kids who use the park," I said. I wondered if we were really a mob. If so we'd have had no compunction about our counterassault.

"We needed to keep him from going bad to worse," Lucy said.

All five of us showed up at the night hearing. Upon his lawyer's request we agreed to drop charges if the flasher would see a shrink. It turned out he had a wife and an infant child.

I thought again about our mob psychology. Maybe it had come time for me to stop going it alone, for us to do another job. Maybe I would tell my sisters about the watch fiasco.

"I can't take it anymore," I said.

"What?"

I waited until I saw without question the precious gems in my sisters' eyes. The votive candle under an outdoor statue of St. Therese, the Little Flower, flashed amethyst for Madeleine, whose patron saint she was.

"I don't know if they are Patek Philippe, known for their intricate mechanical movements and timeless—pun intended—

designs, or Audemars Piguet, or Vacheron Constantin, hand-crafted since the 1700s. Or plain old Rolex or what."

When I spoke again their eyes were still gemstones. They were all mute. "Hey, listen," I said loudly. "Some hood is strong-arming Dad." Four pairs of eyes, a drop of blood in each one, looked at me.

"Who?" one of my sisters asked.

"What are you talking?" Lucy asked. "Where?"

"Hot watches. At Dad's business. We need to get together and do something about hot watches."

"She's speaking in tongues," Rena said.

"You channeling Madeleine again?" Maria asked.

"They're going to bring heat to our family and Dad and his clean business."

I started from the beginning, going back to early November, barely three weeks ago. I told them the whole story blow by blow, starting with the watch tossing, and how Sam Bono owned Dad's land and had him over a barrel. How Sam was now allegedly dead. How I don't know exactly where the watches were, but figured we could find them, hock them, and use the money for the Mariners Mansion restoration.

The most amazing thing was that they did not interrupt me once. I believe they were mostly astonished that I had kept the story to myself and not come to them until after I had done a bit of research. But I could tell by my sisters' eyes and calmness that they wanted to act.

Sure enough, as soon as I finished Lucy said, "We gotta do something!"

"I agree, but what can we do?" said Rena. "Going to the police is not an option?"

"I thought of that—who's gonna believe that Dad, Sicilian and goombah, didn't know or want the watches?"

"Dad's just been burying his head in the sand?"

"Dad, an ostrich?"

"Well, I think he's recalling when the mob strong-armed his father into storing moonshine during Prohibition. They told him it was flour and Grandpa suffered no consequences. I think the local constable was paid off back then. Get my drift?"

"What? Pay off the police?"

"No, not today. This ain't your garden-variety sex perv, that'd be a cinch," Rena said.

"Agreed. Let's just get the watches out of there first. Then we can decide the next step."

"Maybe we should hire a lawyer," Lucy suggested.

"We don't do lawyers," I said. "Pay one to do what we can?"

"Yeah, it's called a consigliere," Maria said.

"You see too many Mafia movies," I said.

"Where we gonna put the goods?" Teresa asked.

"Okay, I was thinking Lucy's but too many kids . . . my apartment on Roselle Street in Linden. My Puerto Rican landlady wouldn't mind even if she knew. She loves me since I painted the apartment in peachy salmon, royal blue, and deep lavender. She's crazy about the rich hues."

"Loving colors doesn't mean she's gonna love harboring hot merchandise," Maria or Teresa said, as my mind raced forward.

I thought about our four brothers—scientist, dancer, inventor, and straight-laced restaurateur—who would never dream of settling Dad's conflict the way we did, who would abide by the book and established precepts. Who would categorically write off any Black Hand business as fanciful, belonging to the realm of myth. I knew my sisters and I could handle this. I wondered why I had waited so long to bring them in. Onward!

We didn't want to send anyone a Black Hand letter. We just wanted to get the hot merchandise off Dad's property. After we agreed to do something, the five of us headed out for a stroll on the boardwalk to enjoy the mild fall day. I stared at the crashing waves, my own sense of pending closure ebbing and flowing with them, a dull pulsing throb. I saw a dolphin raise its head but it turned out to be a wet suit attached to a surfboard. I'd read that the ancient Greeks believed dolphins transported the dead to the next reality, and today the creature meant rebirth, an ability to handle rough waters. A good sign for us.

Sunday, November 24

I sat at Grandma Coniglio's kitchen table with my sisters, Lucy, Rena, Maria, and Teresa. It was not quite full moon, four days before Thanksgiving. They had been meeting at the full moon since shortly after Madeleine's death. Eventually, I was old enough to join them. We always lit a votive candle and invoked her baptismal name, all of her names, including that of her patron saint. "Blessed are the fruits of Magdalena Maria Therese, our sister Madeleine Donitella, may her spirit dwell among us, now and forever, as it was in her beginning and will be for eternity, so be it." This time I added, "Sister Madeleine, guide our endeavor through to completion. In your eternal purity bless our secret heist to rectify an unpure heist. So be it."

"The waxing moon could be either auspicious or inauspicious for stealing stolen goods," Lucy said.

I thought, *Let the silver light be that radiance that shone down on Mom and Dad that summer, that Sunday, the evening the spirit of Grandpa Donitella changed cheese to gold and "Stardust" filled their world, perhaps the whole world. And Grandpa Donitella ate the Last Cannoli from the beyond.*

Mom, Dad, Vinnie, Dana, Frankie, and Carmine were shopping and preparing a few of the do-ahead dishes for Thanksgiving. Like so many previous years, the feast was supposed to be in our cellar. I wondered how we'd all fit as more and more relatives were expected. Sister Julieta would take the train in from Manhattan to join us.

My nervous stomach could hardly imagine the tons of food we'd have: antipasto with Dad's homegrown fennel, cheese-stuffed ravioli, Vinnie's homemade sausage, Dana's braciola, turkey, stuffing, and gravy, Frankie's stuffed mushrooms, Mom's home-baked pies—extra coconut custard, lemon meringue, her special cassata this year—and all the various pastries from Bella Palermo, down to the cannoli. If anyone was prone to *acidita,* this feast would do it in grand style.

I was most looking forward to the ritual blessing of the Last Cannoli. That frozen relic was a miraculous model of preservation. Even when other foods in the freezer went south, the Last Cannoli kept its soul.

But before then, we would be breaking into our own father's business. We piled into one car and parked a block away. I had keys to open the front door. The mute rows of fruit and vegetable pyramids in their rainbow of colors, the exotics the Latino population was asking for, all were staring at us like free verse in a poem waiting to be organized into logical stanzas. That's how I saw food, especially produce in its raw form, unshaped into the dish or recipe it begged us to whip it into. Or at least we thought it spoke to us so.

The Italian stuff, the old guard, as always peacefully coexisted next to the standard American vegetables and also, as they reached our shores, the new foods—much like the human immigrants on whom we projected our love or hate, our ambivalence.

Laid out on a long table were one each of new exotics: breadfruit, carambola, cherimoya, feijoa, guava, kiwi, kumquat, passion fruit, pepino, persimmon, pomelo, quince, sapodilla, tamarillo, tamarind, Ugli fruit, white sapote. Food writers had been visiting us lately to take photographs and ask how to use the array of funny-looking new produce. Dad left it to me to come up with recipes for the exotics. He said if it were his choice, he'd carry only the old standard Italian greens, according to seasonal dictates.

An editor from an organic gardening magazine had said, "You are on the forefront of a food revolution." I thought that sounded elite. Food was food. We, or someone else, grew it, harvested it, packaged it, and sold it, but even if we did not have all this variety we would not starve. Look at Grandma Coniglio's little garden patch.

For our nocturnal break-in we wore headlamps, like spelunkers or characters in a Nancy Drew mystery. Our sister shenanigans propelled us forward in a daisy chain of hand-holding in the dark, bursting into nervous laughter, sneezing at the chill. We joked about getting in with the local mobs who needed help with heists. Making them deals they couldn't refuse.

"I'm sure this is how not to do it," I said.

Once inside we tackled the walk-in refrigerator that I thought was always locked. Surprise, it was not really locked. All we had to do was pull up and down on the padlock, and bingo, it opened. We searched the fridge carefully, moving crates, feeling along the walls for secret compartments. No luck.

We sighed, scratched our heads, mumbled this and that. I thought a minute or two. "Well there is the shed out back where we put trash and recyclables. Might be critters, raccoons and such to deal with. But we've gone this far," I said.

Like a ten-legged sister-pede we inched over to the shed in a single unit. It seemed odd to lock a trash shed but lately intruders had been after the recyclables. Rena brought out the big guns. She had managed to procure the tool we needed, a lock pick. "I ran into an old buddy, Freddie, who used to like Madeleine, tried to date her right before she died—she stood him up one too many times. Anyway, he's a contractor now and I just told him we had a lock we'd lost the combination to. He winked and gave me the tools."

She pulled out a thin piece of metal with a hook at its end and began trying to manipulate the pins inside the lock with it. No luck for a good ten minutes.

"How many Sicilians does it take to pick a lock?" Maria asked. "Don't answer."

"And how long?" I said impatiently.

Freddie had also supplied Rena with something she called a tension wrench. "The basic idea is to apply rotational force to the lock's cylinder in the direction that the lock would turn if the correct combination were used," she explained.

"It sounds like sex instructions for a couple who want to get pregnant."

"I don't know what kind of sex partners you've had . . ."

"Not missionaries, for sure."

Rena grunted and we thought she had it. She recited, "While holding the tension wrench in place, the lock pick is inserted into the keyway and used to lift each pin to the correct height." Every time we heard a noise, someone screeched and she had to start all over.

"Maybe you should not speak as you follow the directions," I said.

"Yeah, it's like one of those Chinese puzzles—as soon as you stop trying," Lucy said.

"Once all of the pins are lifted to their correct heights," Rena grunted again, "the lock will turn and open." Easier said than done. "Freddie said this method requires a good deal of skill, a flick of the wrist, and practice to master, in addition to these specialized tools."

"Maybe we should've practiced somewhere else," Lucy said.

"What, like a bank?" Rena said.

"Yeah, I think we all got new careers ahead. Screw the

mobs. We all go in business together. Call it Five Sisters, Take Your Pick or We Un-Lock and Un-Load—after those Marine guys," Lucy said.

"Carmela, you could be the Cat burglar," said Teresa.

"You guys ain't helping," said Rena.

"How about a wiggle of the butt," Lucy said. "Might help."

"Okay, *mamaluke*, I'm wiggling my butt and nothing's happening up front here."

For a long time all we could hear was breathing. "Ahhh," Rena said finally. "Got it." The lock seemed to click and we heard a mini-explosion of sound. "Success!"

"By the light of the silvery moon," I sang.

We entered the shed. There was a rotting, musty smell— maybe mice or other varmints. Shadows were swirling around from our headlamps. We saw a few crates and boxes and not much else. Until light fell on another door, also locked. This time Rena got the padlock open faster. The small door, flush with the wall, creaked open.

Onto empty space.

"That's where we hide the bodies," Rena said.

"Now what," I said, discouraged beyond belief.

"Carmela, you sure—about the watches?"

"Sure as . . . Shinola . . ."

"Let's look outside again," Rena said, not to be deterred. "We're lucky to have a lot of moonlight. And I'm getting good at lock picking."

"Turn off the headlamps," Maria said.

We looked like the zombies in *Night of the Living Dead* as we spread out around the perimeter, looking for a trapdoor I knew was not there. Rena wandered over to the concrete-block structure and I saw her patting it down.

"Careful," I yelled. "That's hot—electrical stuff."

She was not paying attention, and next thing I knew I was seeing her lit up as if she'd been electrocuted—a fleeting hallucination. In a flash she had pried open the iron door.

"What the fu . . . ?"

We all ran over to her and shone our lamps into the void.

"You may be crazy, Carmela, but you're not loony," Rena said. "Who wants to do the honors?"

There was nothing inside but a huge barrel—the blasted barrel! Rena pried off the lid. Lucy put her hand in and screamed bloody murder. We all froze.

"What is it? A dead body?"

"A dead something. There's a dead animal in there!"

As the others cringed back, I shone my headlamp in the barrel and pulled out a fur coat. Underneath it were several boxes with jewelry, an old-timey watch, rings, necklaces, bracelets, brooches, and a few silver or platinum bowls and chalices. Everything was studded with diamonds or rhinestones and other jewels. I looked closely at one brooch and saw it was monogrammed. It took a minute to decipher the fancy curly letters but I recognized AAA. The fur coat had the same monogram on the label.

"Hmmm," said Teresa. "Triple A, the road service guys?"

My heart jumped or maybe skipped a beat or two. My breath caught, then I released a long exhalation. A synapse had fired in my brain's memory. All that probing of the police blotters was not in vain. Somebody Addis—two first names starting with A.

All I could think was *Dad is no longer over a barrel.
Thank you sister Madeleine.*

The Betty Lind Diner on St. George Avenue. Where else
would we go near midnight on a Sunday to make an
important decision but to one of Jersey's finest 24-hour
Greek diners. We needed to discuss how to proceed.
Couldn't do it on an empty stomach. I knew the goods had
to be connected to the Upper East Side heist I had read about
not long ago. What was Sammy's game? Of course, he had
to come up with a cock-and-bull story about watches. The
fake Rolex. We knew we needed to report this to the
authorities, but what if they thought Dad was involved?

No longer suffering from a nervous stomach, I joined my
sisters in sharing grilled cheese with ham and tomato,
followed by strawberry cheesecake. New York style but
made in Jersey.

"Do we call Dad first or the police?" we wondered aloud.
Each bite of good American diner food brought us closer to
a consensus. Both. As we stared at plates empty of any trace
of food, we agreed we'd return to the produce stand and use
the phone there. Lucy would call Dad. Then I would call the
Elizabeth police and tell them what I was sure was the
case—that some *mammalucco* was using my father's
business to stash hot goods. We all headed back to the
produce stand.

As we pulled up to the front we were showered with the
flashing lights and sirens of a police car. Through a bullhorn

a disembodied voice roared, "Stay inside the car!" Without being told to, we all put our hands up. Then we froze.

The police had gotten there before we were able to call; someone must have seen or heard us and reported suspicious activity. Officer Danny Buttafuoco, who knew our whole family, shone his flashlight in the car and recognized me. He let us get out of the car. True to form all my sisters started talking at once. Officer Danny yelled, "Damn it, one at a time! You girls got me totally confused."

I tried to tell him the whole story. "Please, just call our father."

"All right, all right, all of you. Looks like your parents are arriving. I see their car. I'll get to the bottom of this party yet."

Dad arrived with Mom, who looked sleepy and worried. "What are you girls up to at this hour?"

We all explained at once and our parents understood the clamor of overlapping voices because they had raised us. I was not surprised to see my father's anger and frustration. First, he wanted to know where we found the barrel of goods. When we told him, he was shocked. He too had thought the concrete block was full of electrical wires. I pointed out how the sign reading DANGER, HIGH VOLTAGE was a phony, just like the Rolex with glass gems. When you looked closely you could see the whole flimsy thing was done with Magic Markers, badly shellacked over to keep the ink from running.

Rena revealed that she only risked it, wedging the iron door open, on a whim. "Cat convinced me the goods had to be here and that was the last place we hadn't looked.

Besides I was wearing black leather gloves."

"That wouldn't have been any protection," Dad said.

Suddenly two more cars pulled up. I recognized one of them as belonging to our brothers.

I heard Officer Danny saying, "What the fuh . . ." and Lucy saying, "Saved by the bros."

"Saved by the brothers, my left eye! You told them?! We did the dirty work!" I yelled.

"Why are they here?" Rena asked.

I didn't answer. I saw Lucy's guilty look.

"I felt we needed backup this time. I told them if I hadn't called by midnight, we might be in trouble."

"I'll be careful who I share my secrets with next time," I said, annoyed.

Mario, who had driven up with our other three brothers, jumped out of his car and said, "Carmela, what are you crazy!? Those hoods knock off people for less . . . You could've gotten the whole family held hostage." He was starting to recall my visit to Sammy when Teresa chimed in, "Yeah, these hood types ain't your garden-variety sex pervs we're so good at foiling."

I blurted out, with some bravado, "Nah. I'm onto these jokers."

"In fact," said Maria, "look over yonder."

Officer Danny had been standing aghast the whole time. Now he shone his flashlight where Maria indicated, across the street from us. We all watched as a black windowless van slowly pulled off.

"They weren't shopping for exotic produce. Probably about to pick up the booty we now have," Maria said.

Officer Danny quickly spoke into his walkie-talkie, calling on police cars to look for a 1984 black van and giving the license number. Then he turned to us, the whole family, befuddled.

"So. What is this? Fine time and place for a Donitella family reunion."

We ignored him, chatting in our various huddles.

"Next time, you talk to me or your brothers," my father said somewhat weakly but sternly. "I don't want my daughters getting mixed up in this business."

Yeah, right, I thought. Feeling proud and arrogant that my sisters and I had busted the case, I said under my breath, "Besides, I'm the Cat—burglar!"

"Carmela, what am I supposed to tell Sammy Bono?" Dad said, out of earshot of the police. If he seemed near tears I knew it was out of frustration, not fear.

"Dad, don't you read the newspaper anymore?"

"I been busy with the holiday rush. Why?"

"Sammy Bono is dead."

"What? When? You sure?"

"A few days ago. He had a heart attack in prison. Well I didn't see his corpse . . . but you can find his obit."

It was such a small buried news item and Sammy was really a small-time hood barely worth the little bit of newsprint. I watched my father's face go blank, relax, then calculate, with some measure of peace, what I already knew. He was no longer over a barrel.

The police were busy taking photos and confiscating the stolen merchandise. My sisters took Mom home. Dad and I went, of our own accord but by special invitation, to the police station to give statements. Fortunately, Dad was easily cleared of any wrongdoing. How could he have known the stolen goods were in the supposed electrical box. He'd been at his new venue for less than a year. Like me he believed the danger sign. Even Officer Danny had believed it. City police, go figure.

Gutsy Rena, I thought, *overlooking danger.* Officer Danny thought that Sammy Bono likely would have kept using the hiding place for other heists, before moving the loot to a fence. Or something like that.

At the police station Dad and I told everything. The police questioned us separately in the way they do, to make sure your stories, or alibis, match. I told my half from the start at the Villa Roma, how Sammy said he had found watches and was trying to locate the owner. We got Big Frank, who was working late, to come too and he corroborated our story in a sworn statement. He even brought the phony Rolex.

"That two-bit hood," Frank muttered.

Officer Danny snickered and said, "What, you prefer a billion-dollar hood?"

The police immediately traced the stolen goods to their owner, Aurora Addis. They seemed to have an idea of who Sammy's accomplices might be but were noncommittal. Maybe they were onto Sammy's suspicious death too. Either way, it was all a big thorn removed from my side. And Dad's. The next day I found out there was a silver lining to the whole nerve-racking fiasco.

Monday, November 25

urora Audrey Addis could have been one of those women leave the convent after a few years of strict vows for a freer, more rewarding worldly life, and channel their religious fervor into wholesome ethical living. At least that was the lens through which we all saw her when we visited. Gershwin's *Rhapsody in Blue* came through speakers hidden in walls, ceiling, floor, soft velvety music like her voice.

"Ten—same parents?" was one of the first things she wanted to know about us. Then she took stock of how much we resembled each other.

"Call me Addie—New Yorkers have a hard time with the Rs in Aurora. Been Addie since my teens."

She wore penny loafers, a blue V-neck cashmere sweater, and slim-fit Fiorucci jeans. She was 72 but looked 50 and very natural, very down-to-earth. She had an enviably well-proportioned body, slightly athletic in a feminine way, and a straight spine, clearly disciplined to avoid the usual dowager's hump. She told us she walked three miles each morning through Central Park. Nothing about her betrayed what she called her "pseudo-socialite" status. She managed a nonprofit, In the Groove, that supported groups bringing music, dance, and movement to the underserved in the United States and around the world.

Addie showed us the window through which the misnamed cat burglar had come in. A fire escape, drain-pipe, and stone notches in the brick aided and abetted his nimble climb.

"I like air—who would have thought a little crack in the window this high up . . . Come, look out here. You see? The ledge could easily be reached from the roof, once they figured out how to get up there. By the way, the burglar or burglars apparently had ambitious plans to enter my neighbor's co-op next, but were scared off, it seems."

"They certainly didn't fear heights," Lucy said.

"We've had a rash of burglaries on the East Side."

"Lucky you weren't home—in a way, I mean, if they were dangerous," I said.

"Oh, I'd have invited them to high tea," Addie said somewhat disingenuously, "like you girls. Now tell me all about the Donitellas."

As Lucy, Rena, Maria, and Teresa spoke over each other telling one family story after another, all of which I had heard many times, I considered the burglars. Not dangerous, my eye. Getting details from the police was no easy task. I had yet to prove my theory but I had good anecdotal evidence and strong suspicions. The burglars were either the same two men who paid a last call on Sammy Bono in Rahway State Prison or they had hired some mountaineer to scale the building's limestone façade. Maybe Sam wouldn't have paid them or shared his booty. I couldn't pretend to understand the criminal mind. And why should I? The shady visitors did not bring the proverbial cake with a knife buried in it, but they surely brought Sam something lethal. I didn't know if I had faith in the prison autopsy to show anything more than cardiac arrest. Sam had been a devil, but as far as I could see, a healthy one. Would we ever know? Did it matter?

Addie wanted to give us a sizable reward for recovering her family heirlooms and her mink coat, which she swore she never wore any longer, now that paintballs were in fashion. We demurred. In fact, she was so enamored of us Donitella girls, she wanted one of us to have the mink. We drew straws and the winner was Teresa.

Maria said, "That's a win for me too." They had been wearing each other's clothes since day one, as long as they had been finishing each other's sentences.

Seeing that we were highly impressed with her town house, Addie gave us a tour.

There were two levels plus a loft connected by a carved-wood spiral staircase. Draperies set the stage for light to enter and exit. A prism of color flowed from two oval stained glass skylights. The ceiling on the loft level featured a mural, a parody of a scene from the Sistine Chapel: God's finger touching Adam, only God looked like Gloria Steinem and Adam like Marilyn Monroe. The surrounding putti looked like the four Beatles and Yoko Ono. Light poured in. It was elegant beyond words. We all loved her two walk-in clothes closets. She began telling us how she was moving into the latest punk and bohemian fashion. "When I'm not dressing preppy," she said.

We returned to the bright drawing room where she and my sisters all started talking fashion, dropping names like Calvin Klein, Ralph Lauren, Vivienne Westwood, Karl Lagerfeld, Versace, Armani, Donna Karan.

"Azzedine Alaïa," Addie said. "Have to love someone with my initials. He's Tunisian. A bit too wild for me, but I love looking at his latest creations."

They went on for a long time about clothes and fashion, my sisters oohing and aahing. I zoned out again, still dazed from sleepless weeks of confusion and anxiety. I was looking forward to our Thanksgiving feast.

When I surfaced to listen to the chatter, my sisters were telling Addie all about the Mariners Mansion and Dad's crazy dream to have ten more kids—adopted ones—and start a private orphanage of sorts. Addie thought that was adorable. She said she didn't have children—"But I had a great time practicing." We laughed at her old joke.

"I have a niece and nephew. Kids enough for me. I attribute my longevity to one healthy marriage in my 60s, for ten years—he has passed on—and being child-free. Maybe good genes. French, English, Ashkenazi . . . that's all I've been told."

Lucy said, "Addie, why don't you join us on Thanksgiving? It's an Italian American feast in our family." The rest of us chimed in the invitation.

"Yes, Addie," I said, "you must. Usually we have it at home, but this year Dad's goombah, Big Frank, pulled strings and got us the entire Villa Roma in Linden. There'll be lots of Sicilian and American food. It's the only time of year we serve cannoli."

Addie hesitated, maybe frightened at the thought of a mob of Sicilians. Then she said, "I'll attend on one condition: You take me on a tour of this run-down mansion. If you won't accept a financial reward, we'll see if there's another way to get your father's dream fulfilled."

The five of us made excited sounds of approval.

"For a buck and a ride on the subway!" Rena stumbled through the old cliché. I held my breath and gave a little aspiration,

Dear Madeleine! If I'd had the nerve and the energy, I'd have jumped up and given Addie a huge bear hug.

Thursday, November 28, Thanksgiving Day

What was my old blond desk, handed down to me from Rena's grammar school days, doing in the middle of the Villa Roma?

I had arrived early to help out before some 50 guests poured in. There was music coming from the desk. I should have known. Carmine was hiding himself in plain sight, crouched behind a Christmas tree with a remote. He'd done it again, using old familiar junk to bring forth music out of nothing. How he did it I didn't know. I only knew what he told me—the three things needed, not to create sound, but to bring it out of the womb or cave where it dwells eternally: a source such as heat or motion, vibration, and a medium. Vibrations disturb the molecules in the air, causing them to dance, bump, and grind like billiard balls aiming for our ears and exciting our brains.

In plain talk, Carmine had salvaged one of those old blond desks from St. Mary's grammar school—it just happened to look like Rena's. He used only the top part. He got the roller from Grandma Coniglio's old wringer washing machine. (She finally gave in to an automatic.) Only he could know how he ever tuned metal prong teeth and mounted them to vibrate with the revolving cylinder driven by a clockwork mechanism, which could be controlled by a lever (also from Grandma's washer) or by the remote he held. How he ever arranged the sequence of notes to produce—what else? —"Stardust," no one on God's green earth may ever know. Of course, he attached two small dolls, a bride and groom, who danced to the music. My sisters and I could boast of our recent sleuthing. But only Carmine could summon forth music from thin air.

This was just practice for his new job. Carmine said that after the guests left he would share a remaining jug of Grandpa Coniglio's wine with us and explain about the organ-grinder he was also concocting from old desks and other junk. An organ-grinder with a monkey, too. Someone stop him before he strikes again! "The crank on the side operates the bellows that pump air through the organ's pipes," he started to tell me. I held up my hand. "Too much info. I don't want to know about its innards—I like to enjoy my blind faith in the mysterious workings of some things in this grand universe. Don't ruin that for me."

The noise level was already chaotic though not everyone was here yet. They arrived in dribs and drabs. There were those who spoke mostly Sicilian, second and third cousins and aunts and uncles of Mom and Dad. They picked us out, the Donitellas, for big hugs and singsong messages: *"Come state, che bella/bello."* And more. They were short and dark and lively.

People sat at four long rectangular tables, or milled around talking loud and catching up on each other's lives. Unlike at wedding receptions, there was no special head table. Everyone sat where they liked. The tables were filled with antipasto trays, four kinds of green and black olives, celery, fennel (Dad's recipe), prosciutto, provolone, caponata (Vinnie and Dana's recipe), marinated *god-dunes* (Frankie's recipe), baskets of sesame-seeded Italian bread. Jugs of red wine filled short goblets. Thank heavens, no hot dogs, hamburgers, or the like, as at the Veterans Day affair.

I saw Sister Julieta and Addie sitting at one table and went to say hello. As I stood over them I saw Julieta was showing photos of her orphanage to Addie. I decided not to interrupt as I surmised they were talking business around the Mariners Mansion. Julieta was pointing out the ten children, five boys and five girls, she had picked out to come when the renovation was finished, probably a year from now.

"The children range in age from five to 12," Julieta said to Addie. "Vincent is beside himself. He knows he has to wait for you to arrange the visas."

"Let me see the darlings," said Addie, pulling their photos close to her. "So these will be the first orphans to live at the Mariners Mansion? My, they are smiling, happy, no trace of their losses—or of deprivation."

"Yes, loss of both parents in this plague of times," said Julieta.

"What are their names?"

"The boys are Newton, Alex, Theo, Mungai, Isaa. The girls are Koresha, Winnie, Evelyn, Sara, Mwara."

"Not one *mzungu*," I chimed in over their shoulders.

"Oh, Carmela," Julieta said, turning her gorgeous face to

me with her tinkly laughter, "cheeky as ever!"

"And more grateful than ever, more than I can express."

"Give thanks to God."

"I just might. And a million thanks to you, Addie," I said, "for sponsoring the children's visas. And for setting up a fund through your nonprofit to help with the renovation."

"I am more than rewarded by this endeavor." Addie lowered her eyes as if that were her prayer. "It's just the sort of project I was ready for in my later years."

I bowed and turned away. I saw Mom sitting with LouAnn Harris and my sisters Maria and Teresa, the Siamese twins, so to speak. Mom had called them her "twin-agers" when they were young. LouAnn summoned me close so I could hear her. "Who will get the Last Cannoli today?" she asked with a smile on her face. I played along.

"Well, usually it's Grandpa Donitella's spirit sneaking it when no one is looking." It crossed my mind to add *Maybe Buddy, your brave soldier husband who died too young, will make an appearance, since he loved the story and got to hear it almost the same day he was cut down.* But I knew from Mom that might be a sore point if Buddy had believed the gossip that LouAnn was not faithful while he fought a war.

LouAnn surprised me by saying, "If Buddy's spirit is here tonight maybe he'll snatch the second to last cannoli."

"I better keep an eye then," I laughed with her. "I'm so glad you and Mom have met. You're good for her."

"She's good for me," LouAnn said. "And I got a big family practically overnight."

"Ah, *si, si,* as we say, *mi casa, su casa,* LouAnn."

I headed to the bar where Ralph Giordano was talking to Big Frank. How Ralph got sprung from jail I'll never know. I had to surmise, based on our night at the cop shop, that Ralph was cleared of complicity in whatever Sam Bono had done. And apparently he was safe out of prison.

"*Cara mia! Ch' se dic*," said Ralph.

"Just happy to see you this side of iron bars."

"Me too, slaphappy. Sprung from the can, will have the deed to my land in a few. Your dad, getting his dream . . . sheesh, wreck of a mansion."

"I suppose I can't ask for details, even though it was my sisters and I who sniffed out the goods. Dad made it clearer than anisette"—Frank slapped a shot of that liqueur on the bar in front of me—"he does not want his daughters involved in any business even remotely crime-related."

"Can't teach an old dog new tricks," said Ralph. "That Sammy Bono could sure spin a web of chaos. May he rest in peace."

I spotted Fletcher come in with his wife and look around for a familiar face. He saw Julieta and headed her way. He had agreed to work as chief contractor on the mansion renovation. Hampton would remain as Dad's produce assistant for now. Addie thought it would be a good idea for Fletcher's daughter, the NYU student, to teach the African children when they arrived.

I had seen drawings and plans for some of the envisioned renovations but I also saw the completed mansion in my mind's eye, a jewel of a small château there amid the weeds of old industry, with gardens and gazebos and old trees, on the regenerated soil of Lenape Indians and the various immigrants who followed. I saw it the way I see gems in my sisters' eyes and Old Carmela's. The way I see into the past I was not here for in the flesh.

Speaking of Old Carmela, Dad had set her up in the concrete block structure to sell her *god-dunes* when they were in season. She found other wild edibles among the weeds in the nearby field, including purslane, bitter cress, and chickweed, the last of which could be made into a medicinal tea.

I caught sight of a dessert table over in the corner. A tray piled with Bella Palermo cannoli, a few dozen of them. The touchstone of our family luck. They enhanced my visionary power.

Big Frank was now talking to a man I didn't recognize who was sitting on a stool, his back to the bar. Big Frank caught my eye and beckoned me over with a nod of his head. He introduced me to Max and we shook hands. I got nervous because of his dark glasses and the stereotypical refined hood appearance, gold rings, gold chain, and thick diamond-studded ID bracelet.

"Nice suede," I uttered nervously, eyeing his fitted buff jacket with its fur collar.

"Armani, one of your people," he says.

"No, he's northern."

Max took off his glasses and rolled his eyes. They were green-blue, like Tony Curtis's. "I won't keep you, just wanted to say hello, here's my card. If your father ever needs my services, I'm at his beck and call."

"Max Fine," I said. "Jewish?"

"Like some of your best friends . . . Married to a Sidgie."

I hadn't heard that shorthand in a long time. "*Sicci* by association."

"Guilty as charged—she's a Bonnano, no relation."

"Hmmm. What's your business?"

"Exterminator. We use pet- and food-safe methods. No muss, no fuss."

"I'll give your card to Dad."

"Tell him he's on our preferred client list." Max got up to leave. "Gotta tend to some *mishigas*."

"Mish . . . Some kind of pest?"

"Yeah, endemic to New Jersey."

"Oh. Sure."

I couldn't help but stare at his chains and rings. He held his left hand out for me to admire. "High-karat ice. Don't worry, it's legit. Not hot."

"It's quite stunning." Like a surreal character who had just crashed the gate, he drifted away. After he was gone I studied his card's fine print: FINGERS FINE, NO JOB WE CAN'T HANDLE.

Big Frank whispered, "He was *not* a friend of Bono's."

I was not sure what to make of Max, but I wanted to mingle with family.

Soon two long tables would groan under the weight of big tureens of ravioli, dented pots of gravy, platters of sausage, meatballs, and spareribs, bowls of freshly grated Parmigiano. Since the boys had done all the cooking, my sisters and I would dish out the food and serve everyone the first course.

Then we would eat some crunchy finocchio for digestion,

wait a few hours, and sit back, knowing there was more to come on this best feast day of the year, a brilliant hybrid of Italian reverence for food and American veneration for the first Thanksgiving—even as that piece of history unraveled, revised with the buried grief of Indians coming to the fore. That's what happens when you don't talk about wounds.

Meanwhile, we ate. We danced and listened to music. Mario was playing "Cow Cow Boogie" on the piano as Vinnie and Dana showed off their new steps. Dad and Mom joined them and they were smiling. Dad, who was drinking only soda water and lime, looked happy and relaxed. I was so glad he hadn't stayed mad at me for long. Fletcher and his wife got up and danced too. Soon others joined in, little kids try to copy adults. Mario played "Stardust" and everyone cleared the floor except Mom and Dad. I might have been the only one to see the silver shaft of moonlight shining down on them. I glanced at a bowl of grated Parmigiano and saw it as flakes of gold.

Dad whispered something in Mario's ear. Cousin Bernie took out his accordion and he and Mario played the tarantella, which made everyone get up to dance like people bitten by tarantulas, laughing as we bumped into each other. No one really knows the exact right way to do this Sicilian folk dance. Next Mario played "Mack the Knife," "The Impossible Dream" (his tribute to Dad), "Volare," then old Italian folk songs. Those who knew the words sang loud to "Eh Cumpari," "Funiculi, Funicula," and "Quel Mazzolin di fiori." Everyone was intoxicated either by wine or by the ambience or by the angels that only some of us could see in the room.

Soon it was time to bring out the roasted turkeys, the stuffing, the sweet potatoes, the stuffed mushrooms, Frankie's breaded *god-dunes*, the brown gravy, the garlicky greens, and the salad. And we would eat again, American style this time. Somewhere into the night, desserts would appear on the table. People would sit around, some on the banquettes at the edge of the room, nodding out.

An aunt asked me, "How's Dean?"

"Fine, he'll be home in January."

"When will I dance at your wedding?"

"You know my smart-aleck answer," I said as I moved away. It was near the end of the evening. I followed my mother through the swinging doors into the industrial-size kitchen where she was wrapping up a cannoli.

"What? The Last Cannoli?" I asked her.

"Oh, there are a few more for the guests who aren't sick yet."

"Why don't you take more?"

"Only need one."

"Why?"

"To replace the one in the freezer."

"What?"

"Don't you know?"

"I guess not. You mean the one that's been in the freezer since 1941?"

"Carmela, you're old enough to know. We always replace the cannoli in the freezer with a fresh one, usually on Thanksgiving because that's when we have them around."

"You mean . . . that cannoli in the freezer does not go back to 1941?"

"My goodness, can you imagine what it could look like if it did?"

"Yes, I can."

"I think it's been two years since I last refreshed it. Time flies when . . . when you have other stories to attend to."

I watched my mother's hands, those hands that had changed hundreds of diapers—cloth ones, not the later disposables. She placed a fresh cannoli in the center of a square piece of white veil and wrapped it snugly, then covered it with clear plastic.

"That's that for another year," she sighed. Just another form of diaper change.

My mind raced, my heart stopped. At first I was so disappointed. It felt as if I had been robbed of an heirloom, a cannoli that had vintage status, as old and sacred as the Holy Grail. I had lost a family secret, a collective memory.

"Does everyone know?"

"I don't know. I don't think they were as invested as you in its being some immortal talisman. I think they all know luck has to be renewed."

"Well, I'll be a monkey's organ-grinder." I thought, *Yes, the symbol and ritual have always been where the meaning lies. Deconstructed, the cannoli is just a blend of cheese, cream, sugar, flour. Or is it something more, bigger?*

Mom said, "It might be a superstition but we don't want to find out that it's not. You know, skip a year and have things go wrong."

As I was catching my breath after this blow to my solar plexus, I remembered how Mom and I had created the story about Malocchio (Evil Eye) and Faccia Bruta (Ugly Face), two imaginary long-ago ancestors who had a spell of restlessness cast on them by a wicked sorcerer. It was during the time of our family's diaspora following the Vietnam War. We borrowed shamelessly from age-old fairy tales about spells and charms. But in our version we provided the antidote that broke the family spell of separation. That at least is what I believed. When we told the story we turned them back into beautiful people, and everyone reunited for a marriage.

But I was starting to wonder, maybe even to understand something Mario had said about time: how the past is in front of us, the future behind. So who knew for sure what came first, a story or its alleged effect?

I sighed deeply, knowing I'd have to riddle this out for some time to come. I said, "Mom, you go sit and talk to LouAnn. Let me attend to the Last Cannoli."

"*Grazie, cara mia.*"

ACKNOWLEDGMENTS

Copy editors: Raufa Dhyan, Bob Cooper

Sicilian language consultants: Ester Maggio and Nazarena Tuzzolino Maggio

Cover design, interior design by James M Shubin

Publicist: Kaye McKinzie, Quatrain PR

ABOUT THE AUTHOR

Camille Cusumano is the author of the memoir, *Tango, an Argentine Love Story,* (2008, Seal Press) and the novel, *The Last Cannoli* (Legas, New York, 2000). She is the editor of several literary travel anthologies (Seal Press) and has won some acclaim for her short fiction. She has written for many publications, including *National Geographic Traveler, San Francisco Chronicle, Los Angeles Times, New York Times,* and *France Today.* She was born in Elizabeth, New Jersey, fifth of ten kids in a Sicilian American family. She lives in San Francisco and regularly travels to big family reunions wherever they take place—from New Jersey to Sicily, from California to New Orleans and once in the flyover city of Louisville, Kentucky.

camillecusumano.com
Read her latest posts on:
Medium.com @CamilleCusumano
Follow her on Facebook

www.ingramcontent.com/pod-product-compliance
Lightning Source LLC
Chambersburg PA
CBHW071522110726
47908CB00003B/918